Astrid Lovell

SPARK IN THE DARK

Romantasy

Astrid Lovell

SPARK
IN THE
DARK

Romantasy

GLAGOSLAV PUBLICATIONS

Contents

Chapter 1: Ash and Shadow

Ash—that's what my world breathed. Not the gray dust of a cooled hearth, but the acrid, bitter grit of the Gloom Blight. It devoured Etheria relentlessly, poisoning the flesh of the earth and the waters, draining life from everything it touched. In its wake, the Blight left dead wastes where the wind chased charred scraps, and a soul-chilling whisper haunted the cursed ones— creatures that had once been people, beasts, even blades of grass.

Legends whispered that Craydol, our forgotten settlement nestled at the foot of the Gloom Fangs, had once bloomed with apple orchards. The elders still remembered those days, their tales sounding like fairy stories amid our squat homes of rough stone and blackened timber, rooted deep into the soil. But that was before the shadow fell upon our lands, before magic twisted from blessing to curse, from gift to brand.

My name is Elara. My magic—the Life-Giving Spark, as the old healer Moira had called it in reverent whispers, the only one who knew its secret—was a chain to me, not a gift. The power to coax color back into a wilting flower or ease the sting of a scratch held no value here, in a world that prized cold steel and callused hands. Worse, it drew sidelong glances and cowardly murmurs in my wake. In Etheria, those who wielded magic were feared and loathed no less than the Blight itself. I had learned to hide my Spark, to smother it, to feel shame for it like some infectious blight. Sometimes, it felt like just another face of the same darkness.

Today's drudgery was no different from a hundred others. I gutted fish in the back alley of the Sly Fox tavern—a den reeking of despair and sour ale. Only here did Mother Gretta, the proprietress with ham-like hands and a temper to match, toss me a few coins for the filthiest work. The stench of fish entrails and stagnant water had seeped into my skin, my threadbare tunic. It clung to me like a mark of shame.

"Elara! Stop dawdling like a sleepy slug! Lord Reynard's expecting his catch for luncheon!" Mother Gretta's voice rasped from the grease-smeared kitchen window.

"Right away, Mother Gretta!" I called back, forcing my tone to servile brightness, not the hollow exhaustion and gnawing hunger I truly felt. Lord Reynard, our self-proclaimed "ruler," was a greasy sort with shifty eyes and damp palms that always seemed eager to land on my shoulder. The thought of this fish ending up on his plate turned my stomach.

It was in that moment, as I scraped away the last stubborn scale, that the ground trembled. A faint vibration, as if some colossal beast far in the mountains had sighed in its sleep. The chickens in their coop clucked in panic. I froze, knife hovering in my hand.

And then the sky fell.

As if some unseen hand had draped black velvet over the sun. The world plunged into ominous twilight. An icy chill slithered beneath my tunic, setting my teeth to chattering. Folks in the square stood like statues, their faces upturned to the darkened heavens, twisted in primal terror. Everything fell silent. A deafening hush pressed down on the settlement, heavy as stone.

And in that deathly quiet came the thunder of hooves.

Steady, heavy, inexorable. Each beat pulsed in my chest like an alarm. From the shadows at the north gate rode five horsemen, woven from darkness itself. Their armor, the color of burnished steel, swallowed the light, and the eyes of their mighty steeds burned with crimson fire. They carried the chill of the grave.

But they weren't what seized my gaze.

At their head, astride a stallion blacker than night, rode he. Lord Kaeden.

A name uttered in whispers across Etheria. Synonymous with the merciless might of Nocturne, the dark citadel at the heart of the Gloom Fangs. The Overlord's right hand, whose legions turned lands to ash. They said his heart was forged of ice, and shadow itself coursed through his veins.

He towered in the saddle, his presence radiating unyielding will—a tangible pressure that weighed on the air. Raven-black strands framed a face sculpted by glaciers: sharp cheekbones, lips set in grim resolve. But his eyes... even from across the square, I felt their frosty power. The hue of storm clouds laced with steel, piercing straight through. At his hip rested a sword in ebony scabbard; its hilt, inlaid with stones the color of con-gealed blood, drank the light, thickening the gloom around it.

He reined in before the tavern. The silence in the square thickened to the point of cracking. Even Mother Gretta froze on the threshold, her face ashen-gray.

Lord Kaeden slowly swept his gaze over the stunned crowd. His thin lips curved in a cold, predatory smirk. When he spoke, his voice was low and velvety, edged with steel that sent a shiver racing down my spine.

"I'm looking for a girl," he said, each word echoing in the hush. "Her name is Elara."

My heart stuttered, then hammered so fiercely I swore the whole square could hear it. The fish knife slipped from my numb fingers, clattering against the stones. Every eye—frightened, curious, gleeful—snapped to me. I felt stripped bare before an unrelenting fate.

Lord Kaeden lazily followed their stares. His icy, penetrating eyes locked onto mine. And in that instant, I understood with paralyzing clarity: the ash my world had breathed was merely a prelude. The true shadow had just come for me.

Blood drained from my face. Instinct lifted my chin.

"You've made a mistake, milord," my voice came out steadier than I felt, though I trembled inside. "My name is... Lina."

The lie tumbled out. Foolish. Futile.

The corner of his mouth twitched, like a predator savoring the final, doomed twitch of its prey.

"Lina?" he drawled, a silent laugh sharpening the velvet of his tone, keen as an ice shard. "The one so desperately trying to hide the scent of fish and fear? The one whose fingers tremble so she can scarcely conceal behind her back her... " He paused, tasting the words. "...Life-Giving Spark?"

It hit me like a blow. That name... only Moira knew it. How could he? Icy dread locked my mind.

"There she is, Your Grace! Elara!" Mother Gretta simpered, shoving me forward. "Ungrateful chit! If you want her, take her—we've nothing but trouble from the girl!"

Lord Reynard was already scurrying toward Kaeden, bowing low in obsequious fawning. "Lord Kaeden, what an honor! If this wench has caught your eye, we wouldn't dream of standing in your way!"

Kaeden didn't spare them a glance. All his attention, heavy as molten lead, pinned me in place. He dismounted with fluid grace, panther-like. He was taller than he'd seemed in the saddle; beneath the black doublet, the muscles of a warrior shifted. He smelled of ozone, cold iron, and something sharp, like thunder over scorched earth.

He took a step toward me. Another. I wanted to flee, but my feet rooted to the ground.

"Elara," he said my name like he was savoring it. "You'll come with me."

It was a command, forged in steel.

"I... won't go anywhere with you," I breathed.

One of his warriors menacingly gripped his sword hilt, but Kaeden halted him with a casual flick of his hand, never breaking that terrifying gaze from mine.

"You will," he repeated, softer now, the quiet laced with more menace than any shout. "Your Spark is needed by my Overlord. And he will have it. Either you come willingly, sparing your life and this... " He disdainfully surveyed the square. "...godsforsaken village. Or Craydol learns today what true Blight means—the kind that arrives with fire and unspeakable horror, at my word alone."

Ice gripped my heart. I glanced at the frozen faces of the people I'd known all my life. At the children huddling against their mothers in fear. I knew he wasn't bluffing. His Overlord. The Dark Sovereign of Nocturne. My Spark... was it truly that vital?

A bitter lump rose in my throat. No choice. My freedom for the lives of dozens.

"Very well," I whispered, angrily brushing away the hot tears of helplessness. I wouldn't give him the satisfaction. "I'll go. But you leave Craydol in peace."

Kaeden tilted his head slightly, appraising my swift surrender. A flicker of cold approval glinted in his eyes.

"Prudent," he said curtly. Then, to the warrior with the scar slashing across his face: "Cassian, ready a horse for her. And see she causes no... trouble."

The last word dripped with frost. To him, I was merely an inconvenience.

Cassian, silent as stone, seized my elbow. His grip was iron, brooking no escape. They led me to the horses. I cast a final glance at Craydol. The people averted their eyes. No one spoke. Only little Timmy, the baker's boy whose bruises I'd secretly mended with my Spark, watched me with wide, frightened eyes, clutching his wooden horse.

They hoisted me onto a mare with restless eyes. Lord Kaeden was already mounted, his dark silhouette looming ominously against the sky, which was beginning to lighten. He gave a sharp signal, and the riders moved out in silence toward the north gate, into the Wastes.

I didn't look back.

We rode in silence. Only the thud of hooves and creak of leather broke the hush. The path led north, toward the jagged peaks of the Gloom Fangs, beyond which lay Nocturne—the city of eternal night.

When Craydol vanished behind a hill, I stole a glance over my shoulder. Far in the distance, only a thin wisp of smoke curled from the tavern's chimney. My former home. My old life.

I faced forward again. Lord Kaeden rode just ahead, his back ramrod straight, unyielding. He paid me no mind, as if I were not a person but prized cargo.

Or perhaps he knew already. Knew all my fears, all my pain. And didn't care.

My Life-Giving Spark... what did they want with it? I had no answers. But one thing I knew for certain: I wouldn't break. I'd find a way to survive. The Spark within me wasn't just for fading flowers. Perhaps it could kindle a fire in my soul. And one day, I'd make Lord Kaeden regret the day he came for the girl named Elara.

The sky above us cleared, but the shadow of his towering figure trailed me, draping me in its chill darkness.

Chapter 2: Breath of the Wastes

The first hours of the journey drowned in oppressive silence. It was broken only by the thud of hooves against parched earth and the ominous cawing of ravens wheeling in the faded sky. They were the only creatures at ease here—black harbingers of doom, trailing our band like shadows. Craydol had long vanished behind a ridge of hills, and with every step, the land grew wilder, scorched to its very core.

Sparse grass gave way to thorny scrub, clawing at scatters of stones cloaked in lichen the color of crusted blood. These were the fringes of the Wastes—lifeless expanses where the Gloom Blight held unchallenged sway. I tried not to look aside, but my gaze snagged on blackened tree skeletons and the bleached bones of unknown beasts.

The scarred warrior, Cassian, still led my mount. He rode beside me, silent and stern, holding my mare's reins. His seamed face was a map of battles endured. The Gloom Fangs loomed on the horizon now, a menacing ridge like the jaws of some ancient monster. Kaeden headed the group, his back straight as a blade, the epitome of unshakeable certainty. He never once glanced back, yet I felt his presence in every fiber of my being, as if an invisible thread bound me to him.

The pallid sun climbed higher, but its rays lost their vigor upon touching the cursed ground. The heavy air carried a rotten, cloying sweetness—the breath of the Blight. It churned my stomach, pressing a weight upon my chest.

We passed the remnants of a village. Only charred husks of homes remained, with a lone chimney jutting forlornly skyward. Not a soul stirred. The wind alone wailed through empty window sockets, keening a dirge of desolation. A shiver ran through me. Was this what lay beyond Craydol's borders? The whole world reduced to ash and ruin?

By midday, thirst clawed at my throat, unrelenting. Dust kicked up by the hooves scraped like sandpaper. My waterskin lay abandoned in Craydol, discarded with the shards of my old life. Beg these soulless agents of shadow? I bit my lip until I tasted blood. Pride was all I had left.

"Here," came Cassian's gravelly voice. He extended a weathered leather flask.

I looked up at him, startled. His face betrayed nothing.

"Thank you," I whispered. The water was tepid, tasting of hide, but it felt like a gift from the heavens.

"Lord Kaeden doesn't want his prize suffering before we reach Nocturne," Cassian explained flatly, retrieving the flask.

His prize. Captive, that's what I was. A valuable trinket for his Overlord. I stole a glance at Kaeden. He was issuing orders to the scouts, every gesture radiating unbreakable command. He seemed less man than flawless engine of steel and shadow. And yet, something in that strength stirred not just fear in me, but a strange, reluctant admiration. He was my enemy, but he was a leader. Therein lay his terrifying allure.

By evening, we halted in a concealed hollow. The warriors kindled a smokeless fire in utter silence. They tossed me a strip of jerked meat—tough as boot leather—and a hunk of stale bread. I ate like a cornered animal among predators.

As twilight deepened and the sounds of the Wastes night grew louder, I steeled myself. The gnawing unknown drove me on. Gathering the remnants of my courage, I approached

Kaeden. He sat apart, methodically honing his long sword. His movements were precise, hypnotic.

"Lord Kaeden," I called, willing my voice not to quiver.

He raised his head with deliberate slowness. In the half-light, his eyes were abyssal wells, firelight dancing in their depths.

"What do you want, Elara?" His even tone carried icy impatience.

"I want to know," I said, clenching my fists. "Why me? What do you plan to do with my Spark?"

He set the sword aside. A cold mockery flickered in his gaze. "You think the fate of a Craydol chit is so vital that I'd reveal my Overlord's designs to you?"

"If my magic is what he needs, then I'm important," I shot back, surprised by my own defiance. "I'm not a thing! I have a right to know what's coming!"

Kaeden's laugh was dry, sharp as cracking ice. "A right? Amusing. Your only right now is to breathe while I permit it. And to obey." He paused, his stare drilling into me. "But very well, I'll sate your curiosity. In part. Your Spark is a key. A key to power that could turn the tide of war. Perhaps even remake this dying world."

A key? My useless magic? It sounded absurd.

"But... I can't do anything," I stammered.

"You'll learn," he cut in, his voice hardening like forged steel. "Nocturne has masters who can awaken any power. Or else..." He paused, his eyes glinting with peril. "...you'll die trying. You never had a choice."

He resumed sharpening the blade, signaling the end.

I stood stunned. Within me lay a key to something vast and terrible. And this frozen lord meant to wrench it free, whatever the cost.

Night fell over the hollow, bringing a piercing chill. I shivered, wrapped in the prickly blanket, but not from the cold—from Kaeden's words and the yawning void ahead.

Suddenly, a shrill, inhuman howl shattered the quiet. It came from perilously close. One of the scouts leaped to his feet.

"Tainted!" he rasped.

In the next breath, three twisted creatures burst from the underbrush. They resembled starved wolves, but their fur hung in ragged clumps, exposing suppurating sores, and their eyes blazed with ravenous red fire. The stench of decay and darkness rolled off them.

Kaeden's warriors formed an iron ring around me in an instant. The lord himself was on his feet before the shout, sword already drawn. He moved with inhuman speed, intercepting the first beast.

The fight was brief and ferocious. Only the Tainted's snarls and the clash of steel pierced the night. The warriors fought like a single machine, each strike precise and lethal. I huddled against a tree, heart pounding in my throat. One of the creatures, flung aside by Cassian's blow, tumbled straight toward me. Its hate-filled eyes locked on mine. It lunged.

I screamed and thrust my hands out on instinct. In that moment, something hot and familiar ignited in my chest, surging through my palms in a scorching wave.

The Tainted, jaws gaping for my throat, let out a startled yelp and reeled away as if struck by an invisible ram. It slammed against a tree trunk with a dull thud and went still, its crimson eyes dimming to nothing.

It happened so fast I barely grasped it. I stared at my trembling hands. What had that been?

A dark silhouette loomed before me, eclipsing the moonlight. Lord Kaeden. The skirmish was over. Dark Tainted blood gleamed on his sword. He glanced at the beast at my feet, then at me. His eyes narrowed, and in their frozen depths, a new spark ignited—sharp, appraising... and wary.

"What," he said softly, enunciating each word like a blade's edge, "was that?"

I had no answer. I didn't understand it myself. And I was afraid—not just of him, but of what stirred inside me.

Chapter 3: Echoes
of the Dead Winds

Kaeden's icy gaze bored into me, probing for answers I didn't possess. Shadows from the dying embers danced across his face, sharpening his features into something feral. The silence rang in my ears, thick and suffocating.

"What," he repeated, each word hammered out like a nail, "was that?" His voice was low, almost a whisper, rendering the threat in it all too tangible.

"I... I don't know," I whispered, my voice betraying me with a tremor. "It lunged at me. I was scared... I was just defending myself."

"Scared?" Kaeden took a slow step closer, and I recoiled instinctively, my back pressing against the rough tree trunk. The other warriors stood frozen, watching in silence. Cassian scowled at the dead creature, and for the first time, I caught in his eye not just stern resolve, but a keen curiosity laced with unease. "The Tainted don't fly backward from a girl's fright, Elara. Don't try to fool me. I've seen enough magic to tell accident from power unleashed."

"I'm not trying to!" I burst out, desperation lending me boldness. "I can't control it! It just... happens!" I swiped angrily at the unwelcome tears stinging my eyes.

He studied me for a long moment, his piercing stare weighing every syllable. It felt as if he could see straight through to my soul. At last, he nodded slowly, as though a decision had settled in his mind.

"So the Spark within you burns brighter than we thought," he murmured, more to himself than to me. "Or you lie better than you seem." He met my eyes again. "Either way, it changes the game. Until Nocturne, you'll ride at my side. And no tricks. Any uncontrolled flare, any attempt to wield your power without my command... and I'll see to it personally that you never cast a spell again. Ever. Do you understand?"

I swallowed hard, a chill dread clamping around me. The threat was no idle one. I could only nod mutely, words failing me.

The rest of the night passed in sleepless torment. My Spark could do more than mend—it could kill? My thoughts tangled in confusion. I'd always seen my magic as something gentle, luminous. But what had surged from me... that was wild. Primal. And Kaeden expected something from me, something beyond my grasp.

At dawn, we set out once more. Now I rode beside Kaeden, and it was exquisite torture. His silent presence bore down on me, forcing me to measure every breath. I felt his brief, appraising glances like touches. I tried not to look at him, but my eyes betrayed me, drifting to the stark line of his profile, to the strong hands gripping the reins. Each time, a poisonous brew stirred in me—fear, hatred, and something more, forbidden and frightening: a curiosity about the very essence of the darkness he embodied.

We pressed deeper into the foothills of the Gloom Fangs. The landscape darkened. Jagged peaks, shrouded in clouds, loomed overhead like a monster's fangs. The air smelled of stone, ice, and profound isolation.

The Tainted grew more frequent. Kaeden's warriors met them with ruthless precision. Kaeden himself fought like a war demon, his movements a primal grace of the predator. Watching him, I felt a whirlwind of horror, revulsion, and reluctant awe at his power—a fascination I quickly smothered in shame. He was my enemy. But gods, he was formidable.

During a halt by a mountain stream, I noticed a deep, ragged gash on the arm of one of the warriors, young Liam—inflicted by Tainted claws, inflamed and swollen. The urge to help, to touch it with my Spark, was an unbearable instinct. I took a step toward him, but immediately collided with Kaeden's glacial, warning stare. He hadn't looked up from the map, but I knew he saw everything.

"Don't even think it," he murmured, low enough for only me to hear. His voice cracked like a whip.

I froze, heat flooding my cheeks in a rush of shame and impotent rage. Who was he to deny me compassion?

By evening of the third day, we reached the ruins of an ancient city. Half-crumbled towers, bearing the scars of lost grandeur, clawed at the leaden sky. The wind howled through vacant windows like a mourning spirit. This place reeked of old magic and death.

"The Citadel of Winds," Kaeden said unexpectedly, and in his voice, I caught unfamiliar notes—melancholy, almost wistful. "Once the greatest city of air mages. But that was long ago. Before the Shadow came."

I gazed at the dead city with a shiver of awe. Magic, once a force for such wonders, not a curse?

"We camp here," his tone hardened once more. "The place is cursed—even the Tainted steer clear. But men..." He paused. "...can be more dangerous than any beast."

We settled in what resembled a temple. As the warriors set up camp, Kaeden beckoned me over.

"You saw what your Spark did to that creature," he began without preamble. "Pure life energy, turned outward. A force that doesn't just heal—it destroys what's twisted by the Blight. Ancient texts call Sparks like yours living weapons against the Shadow. The most potent, potentially."

I listened, breath held. A living weapon... was that me?

"My Overlord believes," Kaeden continued with steely conviction, "that such a Spark could purge the Gloom Blight from the land. Restore life to Etheria." He paused, his eyes locking onto mine. "But it demands absolute control. Unbreakable will. And you, girl—you have neither. Just blind instincts and fear."

"But why does your Overlord want this?" I couldn't hold back. "Shouldn't he revel in the Blight?"

A sardonic smirk tugged at his lips. "You know so little. Understand this: my Overlord seeks order. Absolute order. And the Gloom Blight is chaos. Unbridled, all-consuming chaos. It will be eradicated. At any cost."

His words, laced with fanatical certainty, echoed in my mind. Order through annihilation... it sounded nobly terrifying. But the cold in his eyes made me doubt the purity of the Dark Sovereign's aims.

A shrill whistle pierced the air from outside—the scout's alarm. Kaeden surged to his feet, hand flying to his sword.

"Intruders!" a warrior shouted from the doorway. "Not Tainted. Men. Many. Armed!"

Kaeden shot me a swift, unyielding glance. "Stay here. Don't even think of running. Try it, and I'll find you—and you'll wish you'd never been born."

With that, he slipped from the chamber, his dark form melting into the shadows as if he were one of them. From outside came furious shouts and the ring of steel. New peril, this time human. And once again, I was at its heart—alone in a cursed city, amid the echoes of dead winds.

Chapter 4: Dance
of Steel and Spark

The furious shouts and clash of steel shattered the silence, reverberating off the ancient stones. I froze, my heart slamming against my ribs in panic. People. Saviors or fresh enemies? In this dying world, the line between them blurred like a mirage.

Kaeden had melted into the shadows as if born of them, leaving only his command: *Don't even think of running*. Where to? Into the darkness teeming with not just Tainted, but these unknown warriors? Madness.

The sounds of battle drew nearer: guttural cries in a harsh tongue, the ring of swords, and sharp, cut-off screams. Fear's icy fingers tightened around my throat. I huddled behind the shattered remnants of a winged statue when two shadows flickered in the doorway. These weren't Kaeden's men. Their armor—rough leather reinforced with metal—gleamed dully. Beast-masked faces leered from beneath hoods, jagged axes gripped in callused hands.

One of them, massive with a bull-thick neck, spotted me. "There's the little bird!" he rasped, baring yellowed teeth beneath his mask. "The boss'll be pleased. He promised a reward for the girl with flame-red hair."

They were hunting *me*. Panic crashed over me like a wave. I scrambled up, searching for an escape.

"Don't touch her." The voice sliced through the air, cold as frostbite, sending a shiver of recognition—and shameful relief—down my spine.

Lord Kaeden. He materialized from the hall's shadows, silent as a specter. Dark blood dripped from his sword. At the sight of him, the attackers faltered for a heartbeat, then roared in fury, charging from both sides.

It was a deadly dance. His blade parried and struck, an extension of his iron will. Flashes of steel, brief grunts, dull thuds—it ended in mere breaths. One crumpled with his throat laid open; the other slid down the wall, trailing a smear of crimson.

Kaeden loomed over them, his chest heaving, face an unreadable mask. "Cassian!" His voice cracked like a lash. "With me! Clear the east wing!"

And he vanished again, his warriors shadowing him like ghosts. I was left with two corpses and a pounding heart. Kaeden's order—*stay put*—burned in my mind like a brand.

But through the roar of blood in my ears, I heard a faint groan.

It came from behind a crumbled wall. Overcoming my fear, I peered around cautiously. There, curled in agony on the stones, lay Liam—the young warrior. A jagged shard of black arrow protruded from his thigh, dark blood pooling swiftly around it.

Pity twisted in my chest, sharp as a knife. He was my captor, but in this moment, just a wounded boy, as much a pawn in someone else's game as I was. Kaeden's command clashed against my very core. I couldn't stand by and watch him die.

Glancing around, I darted to Liam's side. "Shh," I whispered. "I'll try to help." A flicker of desperate hope lit his eyes.

The arrow had sunk deep. I had no herbs, nothing from Moira's teachings. Only my treacherous, unpredictable Spark.

I closed my eyes, summoning the warmth that had flared the night before. It came—faint at first, then steady, like a stream of liquid light flowing from my soul's depths. I laid my hands gently over the wound, feeling the hot, sticky blood beneath my fingers. With every fiber of my being, I willed the pain away, the bleeding to stop. I sensed his muscles easing under my palms, the blood slowing, thickening.

When I opened my eyes, drained to my core yet strangely serene, Liam stared at me in wonder. "You're... a witch," he whispered, no fear in his voice—only raw awe. And gratitude.

"What in the hells is this?!"

Kaeden's voice whipped through the air like a lash. He filled the doorway, blood still dripping from his sword. The fight must have ended. His gaze flicked from me to Liam, and his face hardened into stone. Fury blazed in his eyes.

"I told you not to move," he hissed, advancing with menace. "I... I just wanted to help," I stammered, pulling my hands back. "He could've died..."

"Help?" Kaeden's laugh was a frozen snarl. "Do you even grasp what you've done, you foolish girl?" He seized my arm, fingers clamping like a vise. "Wielding your power so openly, here? You think this is a game?"

"I didn't think! I couldn't just do nothing!" Tears of hurt and anger scorched my eyes.

"That's right—you didn't think!" His voice rose to a roar, shaking the citadel's walls. "Your Spark isn't a toy, you idiot! It's a weapon! Dangerous, unpredictable! You nearly gave us all away! If those attackers had been from the Order of Purification..."

He trailed off, but the name alone sent ice through my veins. Witch-hunters.

Suddenly, Cassian, who had been examining Liam's wound, looked up. "Lord Kaeden," he said, his tone solid as rock. "The arrow was poisoned. Fast-acting venom. Without her, Liam would've been gone by now."

Kaeden went still. His grip on my arm loosened. The rage in his eyes didn't fade, but something else flickered there—shock, disbelief, and an elusive shadow that twisted my heart in quiet agony.

The silence in the chamber turned deafening.

"Get Liam back to camp," Kaeden said hoarsely, releasing me. "Double the watches. We leave at dawn."

He leveled a long, inscrutable look at me, then turned and melted into the shadows, leaving behind only chill and unspoken tension.

I stood trembling—not just from fear or exhaustion, but from the unbearable strain stretched between me and the Lord of Shadows, taut as a bowstring.

Chapter 5: Gates of Darkness

The night in the Citadel of Winds stretched long and jagged. Tension hung in the air, thick as centuries-old dust. The wind howled through the vacant sockets of windows, while firelight shadows cavorted on the walls in eerie shapes.

They carried Liam to the flames. Cassian, stern and wordless, deftly extracted the arrow shard and dressed the wound with sharp-scented herbs. It was clear: without my Spark, the warrior wouldn't have seen dawn. I saw it in Cassian's gaze— no longer hostile, but laced with superstitious wariness and grudging respect. The other warriors now gave me a wide berth, as if I were some feral beast. They feared me. And that was a strange, intoxicating sensation.

I sat apart, hollowed out from wielding the Spark, but in the depths of my soul—where only fear had dwelled before— something new stirred. Realization. My magic was power. True, living power, capable of defying the dark. It terrified me, but it kindled a desperate hope too. Hope that I wasn't merely a pawn. That I could fight back.

When most of the warriors had drifted into uneasy sleep, Lord Kaeden approached me without a sound. "We need to talk," he said, his voice low but unyielding as steel. He settled across from me, the dancing flames between us warping his features—now a mask of merciless divinity, now the snarl of a beast.

"I'm listening," I replied, my heart quickening.

"You saved his life," Kaeden began, nodding toward the sleeping Liam. There was no gratitude in his tone, no approval—just a stark statement of fact. "But the way you did it..." He leaned forward, his eyes boring into me like embers. "...was reckless. Dangerous. Do you even comprehend the power you hold? You didn't just shove that creature aside. You incinerated it."

"I'm starting to," I said quietly. "But I don't know how to control it. It surges out on its own—when I'm scared. Or when someone's in danger."

"Just surges out," he echoed slowly, his sarcasm cutting like a blade. "Elara, your Spark isn't a gentle stream. It's a devastating avalanche. And you're standing in its path, with no idea how not to drown."

"Then teach me!" The words escaped before I could rein them in. I bit my tongue, startled by my own audacity.

Kaeden arched a brow in surprise. "Teach you? You're asking me—servant of the Overlord of Shadows—to instruct you in wielding a force hostile to everything I serve?"

"You said yourself my Spark is vital to your Overlord," I countered, drawing on desperate courage. "If I can't master it, I might prove useless. Or a threat to your plans. You wouldn't want me accidentally incinerating half of Nocturne, would you?"

He regarded me for a long moment, and a cold, mirthless smirk tugged at his lips. "You're not as foolish as you appear. There's truth in your words. An uncontrolled weapon endangers everyone." He paused, weighing his decision. "I'm no mentor of Light magic. But I know power. And discipline. Perhaps I can give you the basics. Enough to keep you from exploding at the wrong moment. And to make you... more useful."

It felt like bargaining with the shadows themselves. But I had no choice. "What do I have to do?" I asked.

"Listen and obey without question," he snapped. "No impulsive acts. Your Spark feeds on your emotions. Master them, and you'll master it. Now sleep. We leave at dawn. And this conversation stays between us."

With that, he rose and withdrew, leaving me to my thoughts and a small, fierce ember of resolve. I *would* learn. And one day, I'd wield that power on my own terms.

At morning's light, we abandoned the ruins. The band's mood was taut as a drawn bowstring. Liam, pale and weak, managed to sit his saddle. When our eyes met, he gave a faint nod. Kaeden noticed, but said nothing.

The path grew harsher, climbing ever higher. Kaeden tested me relentlessly. When I stumbled, he ground out, "Focus. Your body is your first weapon." When I flinched from a mountain bird's cry, he observed coolly, "Fear is poison. In Nocturne, it kills faster than any blade."

These weren't lessons—they were brutal trials of endurance. But I clenched my jaw and heeded him, seeking the truth beneath his barbs. He was right.

In a narrow gorge one afternoon, my mare faltered on loose scree. I cried out, balance slipping away, but Kaeden's strong hand clamped my forearm, yanking me back from the brink. His face hovered inches from mine, and for a heartbeat, I drowned in the storm-gray of his eyes. No anger there, no mockery—just utter focus, and something else that stole my breath.

"Hold tight, Elara," he growled, voice rough as gravel. "The Overlord needs you alive. For now."

He hauled me back into the saddle with a jerk, as if my touch burned. But the heat of his fingers lingered on my skin long after, mingling fear with a new, unsettling warmth.

By evening of the fifth day, we reached a sheer cliff face. At its base yawned a narrow fissure. "We've arrived," Kaeden said curtly, dismounting. "The Gates of Nocturne. The hidden path to the heart of my Overlord's domain."

Gates of Nocturne. I stared into the black maw of the rock, from which emanated a sepulchral chill, and a shiver gripped me. The end of one road. The start of another, far more terrifying.

Kaeden extended an amulet on a leather cord—a smooth black stone etched with a rune like a frozen spider. "Wear it. It'll mask your Spark. Don't remove it, no matter what. Understood?"

I nodded silently, taking it. The stone was heavy, cold as a shard of night.

"Good," Kaeden said. "Because from here, you enter a world where mistakes don't just cost lives. They claim souls."

He stepped into the gloom, his warriors trailing like shades. No choice remained for me. Swallowing the lump of dread, I slipped the amulet over my neck. The stone settled against my skin, cold and unyielding, and I felt my Spark recoil, stifled by its dark aura. As if a piece of me were dying.

And I followed Lord Kaeden into the darkness, toward whatever fate awaited.

Chapter 6: In the Belly
of the Mountain

The darkness in the tunnel was thick, like a raw shroud of burial cloth. The stone underfoot—damp and slick—sucked at my boots. The air reeked of ancient dampness and something subtly metallic, as if rusted mechanisms decayed in the mountain's depths. The amulet around my neck leeched away the last vestiges of warmth. I felt my Spark, usually a gentle glow in my chest, contract beneath its weight—dimmed, alien. As if a piece of me had been stolen, leaving only a hollow shell.

The band moved swiftly and silently, as if the warriors had been born to these bowels. Only Cassian, bringing up the rear, carried a torch, its flickering light carving trembling patches from the gloom while consigning the rest to writhing, malevolent shadows. I clung close to Kaeden's towering form—not from trust, but because the thought of losing my way in this suffocating maze terrified me more than his frosty aura.

Once, when the passage plunged sharply downward, I stumbled and instinctively steadied myself against his back. He tensed, without turning. Beneath my palm, through the coarse fabric, I felt a fleeting warmth— a shocking pulse of life in this dead underworld. I yanked my hand away as if scorched, my cheeks burning with shame and a sharp pang of confusion.

The journey seemed endless. We threaded narrow fissures, echoing caverns, and a precarious rope bridge spanning a yawning black chasm. Kaeden half-dragged me across it, his grip on my elbow like iron, unyielding against the rising tide of my panic.

At last, a glow flickered ahead. We emerged into a vast subterranean cavern.

I gasped despite myself.

This was a city carved from the mountain's heart. Colossal pillars of obsidian stone, etched with intricate carvings of nightmarish beasts and blood-soaked battles, soared upward into obscurity. Graceful bridges and galleries wove a labyrinth at varying heights between them. Buildings clung to the cavern walls like the nests of raptors, their arrow-slit windows aglow with crimson or ghostly blue magical light. The air hummed with ozone, molten metal, and heavy, spiced incense that dizzied the senses. Nocturne. The City of Shadows.

Its oppressive grandeur inspired awe and primal dread in equal measure. Figures scurried along ramps: warriors in ebony armor, servants in shapeless robes hurrying with downcast eyes. And... something else. With a shudder, I spotted tall, unnaturally slender beings with skin like ash and enormous, pupil-less eyes that burned with inner fire. Even Nocturne's soldiers hastened to yield the path at their approach. The mere sight of them sent chills racing down my spine.

They led us through echoing halls draped in tapestries depicting the Overlord's triumphs, and along twisting corridors. No one spared me a glance—all eyes, brimming with fear and fawning deference, fixed on Lord Kaeden.

Finally, we halted before a heavy door banded in iron. "This is your chamber," Kaeden said, his voice stripped of inflection. "You'll reside here until my Overlord decrees your fate. Any attempt at escape or defiance..." He paused, his eyes gleaming with cold warning. "...will bring the most exquisite suffering. You won't want to test the Overlord's wrath. Or mine."

The room was sparse, ascetic as a monk's cell: rough-hewn walls, a narrow barred window high under the ceiling, a simple bed, table, and chair. My prison.

"Clean clothes will be brought," Kaeden continued tonelessly. "A servant will come to tend the space. Don't speak to her. All your needs go through me. Understood?"

I nodded mutely, a chill despair settling in my bones. I was trapped.

"Good." He turned to leave, then halted. "The amulet," he said without looking back. "Never remove it. It doesn't just conceal your Spark. It... protects you. From certain... entities in Nocturne's lower levels. Ones with a voracious hunger for pure life magic."

He departed. The door thudded shut, the heavy bolt scraping into place. I was alone.

I sank onto the hard bed. My body ached from the grueling trek. I touched the amulet. Protection? Or suppression, rendering me even more helpless? I reached for my Spark, but it felt distant, walled off behind an impenetrable barrier—muffled, intangible. As if my last anchor had been severed.

I approached the window, but the bars framed only a bleak stretch of rock and distant, hostile flickers of light. I was a captive. But I wouldn't yield. Even here, in this city of eternal night, I would fight—for myself, for my Spark, for my life.

The silence broke with a scrape at the door's slot. A gaunt woman's face appeared in the opening, her eyes dull and lifeless. The servant wordlessly placed a clay bowl of watery gruel and a hunk of bread on the floor, then vanished.

I touched the amulet again. Something in Kaeden's parting words— that unexpected, almost human caution—nagged at me.

What entities? And why did my feeble Spark draw them so?

Nocturne guarded its sinister secrets, and I sensed I'd only begun to brush against them. A brush that might prove fatal.

Chapter 7: Whispers
of Stone and Shadow

Days in my stone cage dragged like cooling molasses, blurring into one another. The oppressive silence was broken only by my footsteps on the chill floor and the distant groans of the mountain itself, amplifying my isolation. I existed in agonizing suspense—awaiting a summons, a trial, or an end that might bring release.

Three times a day, the door grated open. A silent servant, her face carved from the same unyielding rock as Nocturne's walls, delivered tasteless gruel and stale bread. She never met my eyes; her movements were mechanical, devoid of life. I tried speaking to her once or twice, but she offered no reply. Her muteness was yet another barrier in my prison.

My sole diversion was the window. Perched on the table, I could glimpse the inner courtyard below: black-armored warriors drilling with unnerving precision, faceless servants scurrying about their tasks. Sometimes, those inhuman figures appeared—tall and gaunt, their skin ashen, eyes vast and pupil-less, burning with an otherworldly glow. Even Nocturne's proud soldiers shrank back in deference. The sight of them sent shivers down my spine, my Spark instinctively recoiling in alarm.

Lord Kaeden did not come. Day one, two, three... I lost count. His absence weighed as heavily as his prior, suffocating presence. I couldn't decide if it brought relief or deeper unease. The uncertainty gnawed at me.

I strained to reach my Spark. The amulet hung like a cold collar, throttling my power. But I persisted. Sitting cross-legged on the floor, eyes closed, I sought that hidden wellspring of light. Sometimes, after exhaustive effort, I sensed a faint echo—like a distant star flickering through dense clouds. It was pitifully weak, but it was hope.

I also began secret exercises. My body, weakened by meager rations, craved motion. Squats, push-ups, stretches—each one ached, but I gritted my teeth. It was my quiet rebellion.

On what I reckoned was the fifth day of confinement, the door swung open, and there stood Lord Kaeden. Impeccable and perilous as ever. In his hands, a stack of weathered tomes. I leaped to my feet, heart racing.

"Missing the outside world, Elara?" he asked with that familiar, icy smirk.

"There's little to occupy me here, milord," I replied, striving for indifference.

"Perhaps this will enlighten your ignorant mind." He tossed the books onto the table with casual disdain. "The history of Etheria. Foundations of the cosmos. And a taste of local lore."

"Why me?"

"Knowledge is power," he said, his gaze cool and appraising. "Or at least a way to avoid folly. My Overlord prefers his... tools..." He lingered on the word, and I flinched inwardly at the humiliation. "...to be minimally informed. Read. You might grasp the perilous game you've entered."

He left me with the volumes and a torrent of fresh questions. I devoured them ravenously. Etheria's history, penned by Nocturne's chroniclers, brimmed with wars, betrayals, and paeans to the Overlord. The cosmology tome spoke of energy flows and the eternal balance of Light and Shadow. The folklore wove grim tales of mages who paid dearly for their wonders. But nowhere, in any page, was there mention of the Life-Giving Spark. I remained alone with my gift.

That night, sleep evaded me. The silence choked. The door—tonight, the bolt's click seemed hesitant. A chance? Or a trap?

I seized it. Heart pounding, I waited until the servant's footsteps faded, then crept to the door on tiptoe. I tugged gently. It yielded with a soft creak.

Unlocked. Or a test? The urge to see beyond these walls overpowered caution. I had nothing left to lose.

The corridor lay empty. I slipped out, melting into the gloom. Which way? I had no map. I simply moved forward, hugging the cold walls, flinching at every whisper of sound. The citadel was a twisting maze. In one passage, drunken laughter echoed. Peering through a half-open door, I saw warriors dicing by lantern light. "...and then Lord Kaeden tells the merchant: 'Your price doesn't suit me. But that insolent head of yours might make a fine addition to my Overlord's collection.' Ha! You should've seen the fool's face!"

A collection of heads... Nausea roiled in my gut. I hurried away.

I wandered aimlessly until I stumbled into a vast, echoing hall. At its center, upon an obsidian pedestal, loomed something draped in heavy, dark cloth embroidered with glowing silver runes. Curiosity eclipsed prudence. I approached and lifted the edge of the fabric.

Beneath pulsed a massive dark crystal, shaped like a diseased human heart. It throbbed with faint crimson light, as if something agonized within. Fissures veined its surface, oozing the

Gloom Blight itself. The amulet at my throat turned to ice, and my Spark fluttered like a caged bird, desperate and afraid.

"What are you doing here?"

The voice—sharp, emotionless, devoid of warmth—jolted me from behind. I spun, heart in my throat. Before me stood one of those ashen-skinned beings, but taller, more ethereal, his form unnaturally graceful in its terror. He wore flowing dark robes embroidered with silver webs. His face was a mask of exquisite, chilling beauty, devoid of feeling. Those enormous violet eyes glowed with ancient, inhuman intellect, peering straight through me—as if reading my soul.

I was caught. And in that frozen instant, I knew with bone-deep certainty: there would be no escape this time.

Chapter 8: Keeper
of Hidden Knowledge

The voice—icy and devoid of feeling—froze me in place. My blood turned to slush in my veins. I turned slowly.

Before me stood one of those ashen-skinned creatures, but this one was different, even more otherworldly. Implausibly tall and slender, he was draped in deep indigo robes embroidered with silver that evoked star charts. His smooth, featureless face held a terrifying beauty in its cold, perfect symmetry. But it was his eyes that mesmerized—vast and abyssal, they glowed with an inner violet light, harboring eons of inhuman wisdom and a chill so profound it stole my breath.

"Who are you, child?" His voice was soft, melodic like the chime of crystal bells, yet commanding. "And how dare you approach the Heart of Shadow?"

The Heart of Shadow... I swallowed convulsively, fighting the tremor in my limbs. "I... I got lost," I stammered, the lie ringing hollow even to my ears.

"Lost?" Irony laced his tone, cold as frost. "Few wander the halls of Lord Kaeden's quarters without purpose. Especially those adorned with such... trinkets." He gestured languidly toward the black stone at my throat. "It conceals your true nature. That little spark of light within you. But not from all. Some of us see deeper."

My heart hammered in panic. He knew. He sensed my Spark, even through the amulet. "Spare yourself the deceit, child," he said, gliding a step closer—hypnotic, serpentine. "I am Morven, Keeper of Hidden Knowledge in Nocturne. I feel the flows of magic as keenly as you feel your own heartbeat. In you slumbers a power. Rare. Pure. And profoundly dangerous. Especially in such unskilled hands."

Rapid, heavy footsteps echoed through the hall. At the threshold, as if conjured from the shadows, appeared Lord Kaeden. His face was darker than night, his eyes flashing with glacial fury. "Morven," Kaeden's voice thrummed like a taut wire, threaded with reluctant respect. "What is this?"

"Lord Kaeden," Morven inclined his head with condescending grace, never breaking his violet stare from me. "I've found your... charge... in a most inappropriate place. She showed an unhealthy fascination with the Heart of Shadow."

Kaeden's scorching gaze pinned me. I shrank back. "Elara, I ordered you to stay in your room!"

"She claims she was lost," Morven murmured, his irony venomous. "But we both know such accidents are rare. Especially for one whose Spark is so... singular."

Kaeden's jaw clenched. "Her Spark is under my control. And protected by the amulet *you* provided."

"Amulets have their flaws," Morven replied evenly. "As does any control built on suppression. Tell me, child—what did you feel when you neared the Heart? Did it speak to you?"

"No... nothing," I whispered.

"Fascinating," Morven studied me with clinical curiosity, as if I were a rare specimen under glass. "The Heart of Shadow usually reacts violently to pure sources of magic. It seeks to consume them... or attune." He turned to Kaeden. "Are you certain she's what the Overlord requires? She seems... too untamed."

"She'll be ready when the time comes," Kaeden snapped. "Her training has begun. And I answer for it."

"Training?" Morven's brow arched in surprise. "You've taken up the role of mentor, Lord Kaeden? Most unexpected. Or do you pursue your own... private aims?"

"I serve the Overlord's will," Kaeden retorted sharply. A spark of icy animosity crackled between them. "Now, if you'll excuse me, I'll return my charge to her quarters."

Morven's smile was faint, chilling—a curve that sent ice prickling down my spine. "As you wish. But I'd advise caution with her. Such Sparks... they're unpredictable. They may unlock power, but they can also become a blaze that consumes everything. Including those foolish enough to try holding them."

With that, Morven glided into the shadows and dissolved, leaving behind a wake of frigid air and unspoken menace.

Kaeden whirled on me. The rage he'd leashed erupted. He seized my arm in a grip that wrenched a cry from my lips. "What in the hells were you thinking?!" he hissed, his face twisting in fury. "Do you grasp the mess you've made? Morven isn't someone to trifle with! One word from him to the Overlord, and there'd be nothing left of you—not even ashes! He'd peel your soul apart and savor every scream!"

"I... the door... it wasn't locked," I whimpered, twisting futilely.

"You *wanted*?" He shook me. "Few in Nocturne can afford to *want*! You've endangered everything! My plans! Your life! And perhaps even the lives of those wretched souls back in your pitiful Craydol!"

The final blow struck harder than any blow. He dragged me through the corridors like a rag doll. At my room, he hurled me inside. "From now on, the door seals with a ward only I or the Overlord can break," he growled, merciless. "And if you dare act out again, I swear by every Shadow, you'll regret the day you were born. Morven's right—you're a danger. And I'm done relying on your so-called good sense."

The door slammed, the bolt clicking, followed by a soft hiss—the ward sealing me in, severing me from the world. Alone, I trembled in terror. The Heart of Shadow... Morven... His dire warning... Kaeden's frozen wrath... It all tangled into a knot of dread.

A blaze that consumes everything... Was that me?

I touched the amulet. It was ice-cold. But now, it seemed to hum faintly. As if something had shifted after brushing the Heart of Shadow. Or encountering that terrifying Morven.

Something had changed. In me. In the amulet. In my fate. And I dreaded what it might mean.

Chapter 9: Lessons of Darkness

The magical seal on the door became another layer of iron bars in my prison. It hummed faintly, releasing a subtle ozone scent—Kaeden's personal brand etched upon my confinement. Isolation turned absolute.

His fury after my escapade left its mark. He didn't appear for several agonizing days, and that silence cut deeper than any threat. I was left alone with my fears and the three dust-caked tomes. I pored over them obsessively, seeking answers. Etheria's history, scripted by Nocturne's scribes, glorified the Overlord's might. But between the lines, I glimpsed another tale—of betrayal, broken oaths, light not extinguished but twisted.

The amulet at my throat behaved oddly. Its cold vibration had become constant. It no longer merely suppressed my Spark; it seemed to engage with it, greedily siphoning fragments of my life force. Paradoxically, I began to sense my power more keenly, more sharply. As if this struggle honed my awareness, compressing the Spark into something denser, more desperate—like a flame whipped by fierce winds.

After several days, the door unsealed. There stood Lord Kaeden in simple black training garb, unarmored. It made him seem even more lethal, like a predator coiled to strike. "Enough wallowing in your pitiful fate," he said, his voice even and glacial, laced with grim determination. "Your training begins today. And I won't coddle you."

Under guard, they escorted me to another, more oppressive wing of the citadel. The walls here were polished black stone; the air heavy with the tang of old blood and ingrained terror. We entered a vast, empty circular chamber. "Here you'll learn," Kaeden declared as the warriors remained outside. "Or break. The choice is yours."

The first "lessons" were exquisite torment. He demanded the impossible—absolute focus, ironclad mastery of emotions. He made me meditate for hours on the frigid floor, straining against the amulet's vise. He provoked me—with barbed jabs at my frailty, tales of his Overlord's cruelties, the horrors of the Gloom Blight. "Your Spark is an untamed blaze," he murmured, his voice slipping under my skin like a blade. "Right now, you're a child with a torch in a powder keg. Learn to wield that fire, or it'll devour you—and everyone around you."

When I teetered on the edge, he grew merciless. "Tears are weakness. Your enemy will strike when you're most vulnerable. You must be like Nocturne's steel—cold, unyielding, unbreakable."

It was unbearable. More than once, I shattered—screaming, accusing him of monstrosity. But he was inexorable. His icy composure infuriated me more than any threat. He'd wait for my outburst to subside, then say indifferently, "We'll continue."

Yet something in me began to shift. I learned to unearth a core of inner silence. One day, when he cruelly mocked Craydol's folk, a wave of blind rage surged within. But I recalled his words on steel. I clenched my fists and... held it. The anger didn't vanish. It still seethed, but it was no longer wild. It became directed. Sharp. Like a blade.

Kaeden noticed. For a fleeting instant, surprise flickered in his eyes, mingled with something akin to grudging approval. But he said nothing.

Days blurred into weeks. The "lessons" persisted. Sometimes we delved into the books, and despite myself, I began to feel... not admiration, but a tangled, aching regard. Primal fear intertwined with reluctant acknowledgment of his keen intellect and that warped, tangible investment in my readiness.

One grueling session, the amulet scorched against my skin. I cried out in sharp pain. "What is it?!" Kaeden was at my side in an instant, raw concern flashing in his eyes. "The amulet... it's burning!" I gasped.

He wrenched it free. The stone blazed hot in his palm, trailing wisps of smoke, its core pulsing with erratic crimson light—the exact hue of the Heart of Shadow. "Intriguing," Kaeden muttered, brows furrowing. "Your Spark is growing stronger. Far stronger than I anticipated." He met my gaze, and in his eyes, I saw a terrifying blend—worry laced with feverish anticipation. "Perhaps you're ready for the next phase."

What did that mean? What new trial awaited?

He slipped the amulet back on cautiously. The stone was merely warm now. But the sense that something had irrevocably changed lingered.

"Tomorrow," Kaeden said, his tone graver than ever. "Tomorrow, we attempt something new. Far more perilous. And I hope, Elara, you've absorbed at least some of my lessons. There's no margin for error left."

He departed, leaving me alone in the echoing chamber with my heart thundering. I knew one truth: the game was escalating in danger. And I, Elara of Craydol, stood at its heart. My will would now shape not just my future, but perhaps the fate of this dying world.

Chapter 10: Kiss
of the Black Lake

The night after Kaeden's words about the "next phase" was pure torment. I tossed on the cold bed, replaying his ominous pronouncement and the amulet's eerie behavior. What did he have planned? Fear tangled with a sharp, aching curiosity. I sensed I stood on the brink of something monumental, something that could reshape everything.

In the morning, Kaeden returned. He carried a bundle of rough cloth. "Get ready," he said evenly, though I caught a undercurrent of tension in his voice. "Today, empty meditations won't suffice. You'll need every ounce of focus. And all your luck."

He handed me the bundle. Inside lay sturdy dark leather attire—snug pants, a tunic, and a sleeveless jacket, plus a pair of solid boots. "Change," he commanded, stepping out but leaving the door ajar.

The clothes fit like a second skin, practical and freeing. When I emerged, Kaeden's gaze swept over me appraisingly before he led the way. This time, we went alone. It unnerved me, yet it carried a heady whisper of liberty.

Our path descended into the mountain's bowels. The air grew colder, damper, laced with stale water and a biting acridity. We passed sealed doors from which emanated odd sounds—grinding mechanisms, muffled groans, and laughter that chilled the soul.

At last, we halted before a massive iron door, rusted and etched with glowing runes. Kaeden pressed his palm to one; it flared with a sickly blue light, and the door groaned open on protesting hinges, exhaling a blast of frigid air and a low, resonant hum.

Beyond lay a vast circular cavern. At its heart gleamed a perfectly round lake. The water was utterly black, still as polished obsidian. From it emanated that vibrating hum and a palpable aura of ancient, slumbering power.

"This is the Black Lake," Kaeden said, his voice echoing off the walls. "One of the few places in Nocturne where Etheria's primal magic still flows in its raw form. It's perilous. The water has a will of its own. It can amplify your Spark to unimaginable heights—or devour it utterly."

I stared at the ebony surface with superstitious dread. It didn't reflect the light; it absorbed it. "What are we doing here?" I asked, a chill prickling my spine.

"You'll learn to truly feel your Spark. Not suppress it, but merge with it. Direct it." Kaeden edged closer to the rim. "The amulet. Remove it. It's a cage for your power. And right now, it needs to fly free."

Take it off? Here? I hesitated. "Don't fear it," he said, impatience edging his tone for the first time. "I'll be here. I won't let the lake harm you. If you follow my lead."

Reluctantly, I unclasped the amulet. In that instant, my Spark—freed from its bonds—fluttered wildly, pulsing with renewed vigor. It flooded me with intoxicating liberty and bone-deep terror.

"Approach the water," Kaeden commanded. "Listen. To yourself. And to the lake."

I inched forward. The black surface loomed near. Its vibration thrummed in harmony with my heartbeat. I closed my eyes and focused.

And I felt it. My unleashed Spark throbbed powerfully, drawn inexorably to the lake. As if it recognized a kindred essence. "What do you feel?" Kaeden's voice came from right beside me.

"Power," I whispered. "Immense, ancient power... And it's... calling to me."

"Good," he said, standing so close I sensed the warmth radiating from him. "Now reach for it. Mentally. Let your Spark touch the lake's energy. Gently."

I drew a deep breath. My Spark, drunk on freedom, thrashed like a caged bird finally loosed. The lake's energy yawned like an endless abyss, ready to swallow my fragile light.

Suddenly, my Spark brushed something. And the world erupted in black light. Thick, viscous darkness surged from the lake, lunging toward me—seeking to engulf, to drag me into an icy void. I screamed, recoiling, but it was too late. The ebony force enveloped me in a suffocating shroud, seeping beneath my skin, leaching my life. My Spark flared desperately, but it was a mere candle against the storm.

"Kaeden!" I cried, clinging to fading consciousness with my last strength.

I saw his face, twisted in an emotion I couldn't name. In those usually glacial eyes, for one horrifying instant, flashed... fear.

Then he did the impossible. He plunged into the roaring torrent of black energy and seized my hands. His grip was iron. In that moment, I felt another power flood through him into me. Not my Spark, not the lake's essence, but something else— fiercely hot, volcanic, cataclysmic as an erupting mountain.

It mingled with my waning light, igniting it, granting it the strength to fight.

Together, our forces struck back at the encroaching dark. Everything stilled. Then the black wave shuddered against an unseen barrier and retreated, slinking back into the lake's placid depths.

I gasped for air on my knees. Kaeden still held me, his face ashen, but his eyes blazed with a wild, manic fire. "Are you... all right?" he rasped.

I could only nod. Exhausted, but alive. And I felt... something had irrevocably shifted. "What... was that?" I managed.

He released my hands with reluctance. "The lake can be unpredictable. Especially with someone like you," he said darkly, eyeing the black water. "Your training just got a lot more interesting than I thought. And far more dangerous."

He helped me to my feet. Now I trembled not just from fear. It was the quake of realization—of the staggering power latent in me. And the even more terrifying, enigmatic force in him.

I understood with chilling clarity: our fates were bound far tighter now. Not merely captor and captive, but woven by this perilous, all-consuming magic that had nearly destroyed us—yet might be our only salvation. Or our ultimate ruin.

Chapter 11: Resonance of Darkness and Light

The trek back from the Black Lake draped us in a silence heavier than the tunnel's gloom. My legs trembled with the effort to keep pace, my body still quaking from the shock. A low hum echoed in my skull, the aftershock of that roaring black wave that had nearly claimed me.

Kaeden walked beside me, his quietude oppressive. His face, usually an impenetrable mask, was pallid and stark, a hard line of exhaustion etched at his mouth. He had tapped into his own power too—that fierce inferno that had saved us both. I stole wary glances at him, but his expression yielded nothing.

We exchanged no words until we reached the empty training chamber. Kaeden gestured silently to a chair; I sank into it, while he dropped heavily into another. For several minutes, he sat with eyes closed, his chest rising and falling in ragged bursts. I'd never seen him like this... vulnerable? No. Utterly focused on reclaiming his strength.

At last, he opened his eyes. His gaze, leaden and unyielding, fixed on me. "Do you understand what happened at the lake, Elara?" His voice was low, stripped of its usual edge.

"I... think so," I whispered. "The lake... it reacted to my Spark. Tried to swallow it."

"Not just your Spark, you foolish girl," he corrected, sharpness creeping back into his tone. "It tried to devour *you* whole.

The Black Lake is a primal font of power. It feeds on magic. And it's ravenous for pure, untamed life energy. You were a lit torch to a starving beast."

A shudder rippled through me. "But you... you used your magic too. Why didn't it—"

"My power is of a different breed," he said flatly. "Forged in shadow, tempered by will. And unlike some, I know how to leash it." He paused. "You don't. Not yet."

"I tried," I said, a lump of despair rising in my throat. "It was too strong."

"I know." The words came unexpectedly soft, startling me more than any outburst. "I underestimated your bond with the Spark. And the lake's hunger. It was my miscalculation. One that nearly cost us both our lives."

I stared at him, disbelief rooting me in place. Lord Kaeden, admitting a fault? To *me*? "What... what now?"

"Direct confrontations with 'living' magic are too risky for you yet. We'll return to the fundamentals. Control. But now..." He lifted his heavy gaze to mine. "...we approach it differently."

"Differently?"

"Yes. You'll learn not to suppress your Spark, but to commune with it. The amulet—" he nodded toward my throat— "will be your instrument. Master it as a shield. A filter. Direct the flow, don't let it sweep you away."

It sounded impossible. But after what I'd endured, I knew there was no alternative. Learn, or perish. "I'll try," I said.

"You won't *try*," he snapped, ice reclaiming his voice. "You'll *do* it. This isn't just about your worthless life—it's about fulfilling the mission my Overlord entrusted to you. And he doesn't forgive failure. Not from anyone."

In the days that followed, our routine shifted. Kaeden guided my meditations, but the focus had changed—to forging a connection with the Spark across the amulet's barrier. He brought fresh tomes: treatises on magic's essence, techniques for mental discipline. Much was arcane, but Kaeden explained with patient precision—his interpretations sharp, cynical, yet uncannily insightful.

In those moments, when he spoke of magic with such depth and fervor, I forgot who he was. But then he'd meet my eyes with that glacial stare, and reality crashed back: my captor, molding me for his shadowy ends.

The strange thread woven between us at the Black Lake lingered in the air. We were enemies. Yet we were also two souls who had brushed the ancient wilds, and that touch left an indelible mark.

One evening, deep in meditation, the amulet warmed against my skin. I felt a distinct pulse—a fragile harmony between it and my Spark. As if, at last, a tenuous resonance had sparked to life.

I opened my eyes in surprise. Kaeden, watching intently, gave a faint nod. "You're beginning to grasp it," he said, a hint of satisfaction threading his voice. "The amulet can be a conduit. An amplifier. If you bend it to your will."

The door flew open without a knock. Cassian stood there, his scar-riddled face etched with unease. "Lord Kaeden," he rasped. "Urgent summons from the Overlord. He... demands your presence. Immediately. And... hers." He nodded warily toward me.

My heart plummeted. The Overlord. The Dark Sovereign himself. He wanted to see *me*. Now.

Kaeden rose slowly. His face hardened into an icy facade, but I caught the dark flicker in his eyes—like the glow of a distant blaze. "It seems, Elara," he said, his tone devoid of warmth or pity, a mere statement of fact, "your first true trial begins far sooner than either of us anticipated."

He held my gaze for a long, inscrutable moment. Then he turned sharply to Cassian. "Prepare her. And hurry. The Overlord despises waiting."

Chapter 12: The Abyss's Gaze

"The Overlord despises waiting." Kaeden's words echoed like frost in my ears as they prepared me for the audience. The icy water they forced me to bathe in washed away not just the grime, but the last shreds of my resolve. They draped me in a dark blue silk gown—a shroud for the sacrificial lamb. My long auburn hair was brushed until it cascaded over my shoulders like a fiery waterfall. The only adornment was the cursed black amulet, pressing against my throat like a humiliating reminder of my dependence.

Lord Kaeden waited at the door. In a perfectly tailored black velvet doublet, he resembled a prince of shadows. His face was impassive, but I noted the tight line of his lips and the flicker of unease in his eyes. "Are you ready?" His voice was steady, but it hummed with coiled tension. I nodded mutely, fear constricting my throat. "Remember everything I've taught you," he said, his gaze sharpening. "Control your emotions. Don't let him see your fear. Answer briefly. And for all that's sacred—" His voice cracked slightly. "—don't try to use your Spark without his command." There was desperate entreaty in his words. "Yes," I whispered. "Then let's go. And may all forgotten gods help us." The last came out as bitter irony.

The path was an eternity of torment. We traversed a sequence of dim, grandiose halls. Black obsidian walls mirrored our quivering shadows. Tapestries depicted harrowing scenes of battles and blood rituals. The air grew colder, the silence more suffocating. Black-armored guards stood sentinel at every turn, motionless as statues forged from darkness itself.

At last, we halted before massive double doors of ebony wood, carved with coiling serpents whose ruby eyes gleamed. Two ashen-skinned beings towered at the threshold—taller and more imposing than any I'd seen. They inclined their heads silently and swung the doors wide.

I held my breath and stepped inside.

The throne room. Vast, endless. The soaring ceiling vanished into obscurity. Smoking braziers provided the only illumination, casting writhing shadows on the walls. At the far end, atop a dais of polished black obsidian, rose a throne hewn from shadowed stone. And upon it sat a figure.

Cloaked in darkness, but I discerned an elegant silhouette. No face was visible. Yet I felt *His* Power—ancient, all-consuming, like a black hole. It pressed down, subjugated, made my knees buckle.

Lord Kaeden dropped to one knee. "My Overlord. I have brought her." I remained standing, spine rigid despite my trembling legs.

"Approach, child," came a voice from the shadows. Soft, caressing—and all the more terrifying for it. "I wish to behold the one who carries such a rare gift."

My legs rebelled, but I compelled them forward a few steps. The enveloping shadow parted. He was no monster. He was inexpressibly, inhumanly beautiful. Long black hair framed a pale, aristocratic face of flawless features. And his eyes... twin shards of the night sky, ablaze with frozen stars. No rage, no malice. Just fathomless depth, eternal wisdom, and... cosmic ennui.

"Elara," he intoned my name like savoring a rare vintage. "Bearer of the Life-Giving Spark. A forgotten gift... impossible."

I stood paralyzed under his gaze. "Lord Kaeden claims you're making progress. Is it true, child? Are you learning to master your gift?"

"I... I'm trying, my Overlord," I stammered.

"Trying?" Venomous amusement laced his voice. "I require results. Absolute mastery." His eyes bored into me. "Show me. Reveal your Spark. Now."

Ice raced down my spine. I cast a pleading glance at Kaeden, but he knelt unmoving. I was alone. "I... I can't, my Overlord. The amulet... it blocks my power."

"Ah, yes. The amulet. Morven's quaint invention. But if your Spark is truly potent... it will find a way. Try, child. Amaze me."

The pressure from him was unbearable. I closed my eyes, summoning Kaeden's lessons. Control. Discipline. Will. I reached, but the amulet clamped my Spark in icy jaws. I pushed again, pouring in my desperation. And felt... a faint, ghostly flicker of warmth.

"Feeble. Pathetically so," the Overlord's voice dripped with disdainful disappointment. "Perhaps Lord Kaeden has over-estimated your talents. Or..." His tone hardened to steel. "...you're simply refusing to obey? You dare defy me?"

"No, my Overlord! I swear, I—"

"Enough!" He raised a hand impatiently. "I have no time for these games. Lord Kaeden!"

"Yes, my Overlord?" Kaeden replied tonelessly.

"Your training progresses intolerably slowly. And time waits for no one. Perhaps she requires different motivation. Morven has long expressed interest in enlightening her personally. He deems your methods too crude for such delicate essence."

My heart sank. Morven? The one whose gaze froze blood? No. Not him. Kaeden stiffened. "My Overlord, she *is* progressing. She just needs more time..."

"There is no time," the Overlord cut him off coldly. "From this day, Elara trains under joint supervision—yours and Morven's. I'm certain it will yield swifter results. Otherwise..." The threat hung unspoken. "Now begone."

He reclined against the throne, his form dissolving into shadow. The audience ended. Kaeden, wordless, gripped my arm and hauled me from the hall. Only when the doors boomed shut did I draw breath. But relief was absent. Only a fresh, deeper horror.

Back at my cell, he spun me to face him with raw fury. "Do you grasp what you've done, you fool?!" he hissed. "Because of your weakness, Morven's now involved! Do you have *any* idea what he'll do to you?!"

"I tried!" I cried, tears of despair spilling.

"The amulet is your only shield!" he snarled. "Learn to wield it, not fight it! Morven won't be as... patient... as I have." Bitter irony twisted his words. "He'll unravel your soul and care nothing for what's left!"

He stepped back, his rage cooling to steely resolve. "We have scant time. Tomorrow morning, Morven comes for you. And by then, you *will* be ready." He flung the door open. "Now go. And pray to every god that tomorrow doesn't make today seem like paradise."

He vanished into the gloom. I was left alone, quaking with dreadful foreboding that the worst was yet to come.

Chapter 13: Whispers of Stars and the Call of Shadow

The morning dawned under a pall of dread. The name "Morven" hung in the air like frost, filling every breath with icy anticipation. Each minute stretched into torment.

When the door creaked open, Kaeden stood there. His face was a mask, but in the depths of his eyes, I glimpsed a shadow of concern. "Morven awaits you in the Western Tower, in his observatory," he said curtly. "I'll escort you."

We traversed the corridors in silence. As we reached the narrow spiral staircase, I couldn't hold back. "Lord Kaeden," I whispered, "what will he do to me?"

He halted, his gaze heavy upon me. "Morven isn't like me, Elara. His weapons are the mind, knowledge, illusions. He'll try to burrow into your soul, dissect your Spark. Don't yield to his words. His deceptive gentleness. Control—that's your only shield." It was more than I'd expected. Advice, almost. "I'll... try," I murmured. He gave a sharp nod. "Go. And be strong." He hesitated. "I'll wait below. Just in case."

The ascent was agony. The higher I climbed, the stronger the peculiar scent grew: dust, aged tomes, dried herbs, and something sweetly spiced that dizzied the senses. At last, I reached a massive oak door. "Enter, child of the Spark," came Morven's melodic voice.

I stepped inside. The observatory was a vast circular chamber beneath a domed ceiling, its center yawning open to the sky, veiled by an invisible barrier. Endless shelves lined the walls, groaning under thousands of books and scrolls. Eccentric instruments of copper and crystal cluttered every surface. At the heart of the room, upon a pedestal, rotated a massive star globe of moonstone, emanating a soft, silvery glow.

Morven himself stood at a telescope. He wore a deep violet robe embroidered with myriad silver stars. "Welcome to my sanctum, Elara," he said without turning. "A place where the universe's secrets occasionally unveil themselves."

He pivoted slowly. His enormous violet eyes gleamed brighter than before. "Lord Kaeden sought to teach you through suppression and fear. The warrior's path. But you are a bearer of light. Your power demands not control, but harmony."

His voice enveloped me, soothing like a lullaby. After Kaeden's glacial severity, Morven's words felt like a healing balm. "Remove the amulet, child," he urged gently. "It shackles your strength." I wavered, recalling Kaeden's warning. "Fear not," Morven smiled, and it was disarmingly warm, kind. "I only wish to help you understand yourself."

Yielding to his allure, I unclasped the amulet. My Spark surged to life with joyous abandon, pulsing with intoxicating vigor. "Good," Morven nodded approvingly. "Now approach the Star Heart." He gestured to the glowing globe. "It will reveal the true nature of your power."

I drew near. Warmth and vibration emanated from the globe, resonating with my Spark. "Close your eyes," Morven murmured. "Feel your Spark. Let it grow. Don't fear it. It is you."

I obeyed. My Spark brightened, warmed, intensified. Fear ebbed away. "Now," Morven continued, "imagine your Spark as a star. And the Star Heart as a galaxy. Let them touch."

Mentally, I extended a tendril of my Spark toward the globe. In an instant, a torrent of visions, knowledge, sensations overwhelmed me. I witnessed the birth and death of stars, the ruin of worlds, heard the music of the spheres. My Spark became part of something infinite. "Yes, child... there it is," Morven whispered. "You feel the true essence of magic... Light... and Shadow..."

But then, amid the radiant flood, a shadow intruded. Cold, viscous. It swelled, twisting the visions, breeding dread. I saw the Gloom Blight devouring Etheria. Saw the Overlord upon his throne. And saw myself beside him, my Spark darkened, serving the void. "No!" I screamed, wrenching free from the trance.

Morven stood nearby, his warm smile vanished. "What was that?" I gasped.

"A most intriguing response," he mused thoughtfully. "You beheld not just Light, but Shadow. That's promising. But why the fear? Shadow is part of creation. Without darkness, there is no light. Sometimes, to achieve a grand purpose, one must embrace it."

"I won't embrace Shadow!" I exclaimed in revulsion. "I saw what it does to the world!"

"You saw only what was permitted," he corrected softly. "And the Overlord... he seeks perfect order. Harmony. Even if it means traversing the gloom."

His words were sweet poison, twisting black into white. "I... don't believe you," I said, meeting his inhuman eyes.

"Pity," he sighed regretfully. "Lord Kaeden seems to have instilled his primitive notions in you. Very well, that's enough for today. Return. And remember: the path to true power lies not in denial, but acceptance."

He turned away, signaling the lesson's end.

I exited, feeling drained. Kaeden waited at the stair's base. "Well?" he demanded sharply.

"Strange," I said. "He's... different."

"I warned you. What did he say?"

I recounted it all: the Star Heart, the visions, Morven's talk of balance and embracing Shadow. Kaeden listened, his jaw tightening, eyes darkening. "He's trying to twist your mind," he said flatly, fury simmering beneath. "Make you believe the Overlord's ends justify the means. Don't listen. Your Spark is light. Pure light. It cannot serve darkness. Ever."

I stared at him in surprise. It was the most fervent thing I'd heard from him. Defending my light. From *him*, the Lord of Shadows. "But why... why do you serve him, then?" I couldn't hold back.

Pain twisted his features. "That's not your concern. I have my reasons. My goals. And old scores to settle—with this world. And with the Overlord." He turned abruptly. "Come. You need rest. Tomorrow... we resume *our* lessons. And try to forget that scheming intruder's words. Or he'll destroy you. And me with you."

We returned to my cell in oppressive quiet. I knew Morven wouldn't relent. And Kaeden hid something. I, Elara of Craydol, was caught between two fires, two mighty forces, each hungry to bend my light to their will.

But now I knew one more truth. My Spark wasn't merely light. It was part of something cosmic, linking me to the stars. And in that, perhaps, lay my key to salvation. Or utter doom.

Chapter 14: Between Light and Shadow

After the observatory lesson, I returned to my cell shattered. The visions haunted me, swirling in a kaleidoscope of brilliance and horror. Morven's seductive words on balance and embracing Shadow echoed relentlessly, striving to drown out Kaeden's desperate pleas for control and the perils of darkness.

My Spark... it was more than mere warmth. It harbored primal might, capable of communing with the energies of the universe itself. The realization intoxicated and terrified me. But the vision of myself at the Overlord's side, my Spark corrupted into shadow... it churned my stomach with visceral revulsion.

Kaeden was right: Morven sought to warp my mind. His talk of harmony was a poisonous bloom. Yet his insinuations—that Kaeden had filled my head with "primitive, soldierly notions of good and evil"—had sown seeds of doubt. What if the world wasn't so black-and-white? What if the Overlord's "order" was the only salvation for Etheria from the Gloom Blight's chaos?

These uncertainties gnawed at me. I stopped eating, stopped sleeping, spending hours in anguished contemplation.

When Kaeden arrived at the training chamber the next day, I was a shadow of myself. "It seems our Keeper of Knowledge left a venomous mark on your impressionable soul," he said dryly, irritation lacing his tone. He studied my face, probing for the doubts festering within. "He... showed me things I've never seen," I replied quietly. "The power of my Spark. Its connection... to everything."

"Morven is a master of illusions, Elara," Kaeden said, approaching slowly. "He can dazzle you with starlight but won't mention how stars burn to ash. His sole aim is to bend your will to him and the Overlord. Don't be fooled."

"And your aim, Lord Kaeden?" I couldn't hold back, meeting his eyes with defiant challenge. "To forge me into an obedient weapon?"

His jaw tightened, a dangerous fire igniting in his gaze. "My aim, Elara," he paused, "is to teach you survival. Survival in this viper's nest. And perhaps, if fortune favors us," his voice softened, "to preserve what little light remains in you."

The words caught me off guard, stilling my heart. Preserve my light? *He*?

Our "lessons" resumed, but transformed. Kaeden redoubled his efforts to counter Morven's influence, pushing me to exhaustion's brink. He brought new volumes—ancient manuscripts of the Light Keepers, which he read aloud with a hidden longing. He spoke of defenses against mental intrusion, the toll exacted by those who dallied with darkness.

"Your Spark, Elara," he insisted, "is not just a weapon, but a shield. A shield for the weak. You could protect, not merely destroy. Heal. Inspire hope. Morven wants to twist it into a poisoned spear—but such a blade can easily turn on its wielder."

I listened, doubts clawing at my soul. Whom to believe?

One day, slumped on the floor in utter fatigue, Kaeden silently offered a flask. "You overthink," he said unexpectedly gently. "And undertrust your instincts. What does your heart tell you, Elara? What did you feel at the Star Heart, before Morven whispered his lies?"

I recalled that all-encompassing ecstasy, the sense of unity with pure light. "I felt... joy," I admitted softly.

"That's your truth," Kaeden nodded with satisfaction. "Your Spark instinctively reaches for light because it *is* light's child. Let no one convince you otherwise. Not even..." He faltered. "...not even if that someone is me."

The door swung open then, a warrior at the threshold. "Lord Kaeden, Magister Illiriy summons you urgently. It concerns... her." Kaeden's brow furrowed sharply. Magister Illiriy—the Overlord's chief sorcerer, Morven's right hand. His involvement boded ill.

"I'll come," Kaeden replied coldly. He turned to me. "Stay here. Don't move. It seems our respite was brief."

He left. Anxiety clenched my chest anew. I approached the table, where an open book displayed an illustration of a Light Keeper's protective rune. My finger traced its lines.

Then the amulet at my throat hummed. But this time, the vibration was warm, yielding. My Spark responded, as if recognizing kin in the ancient symbol.

A vision ignited in my mind. A shadowed hall. A stone altar. Upon it, a girl eerily like me. Hooded figures stood motionless in dark robes. And looming over the altar—Morven. His violet eyes blazed with predatory hunger, a ritual dagger of black metal gripped in his hand...

The vision faded, leaving me trembling in horror. What was that? A warning? A prophecy?

I didn't know. But one certainty burned: time was slipping away. I had to act. Urgently. Before it was too late.

Chapter 15: Spark
Against Shadow

Kaeden's departure left me alone with the vision's chilling grip. Magister Illiriy. The name echoed from the books and Kaeden's tales of dread. Nocturne's eldest and most potent sorcerer, Morven's right hand, master of dark rites. His interest in me promised nothing but ruin.

I replayed the nightmare over and over: the shadowed altar, the girl resembling me bound upon it, Morven raising his ritual dagger. Imagination's cruel jest, or a true warning from my Spark? The amulet at my throat lay cold and inert once more.

Time dragged in agony. At last, familiar footsteps approached. The door opened, and Kaeden appeared, his face stormier than I'd ever seen. "What... what did he want?" My voice quivered.

"Illiriy," Kaeden said hollowly, raw fury underscoring the word. "That ancient spider is preparing a ritual. 'Purification and Direction of Power.' He deems your Spark too 'wild,' too luminous. It requires immediate... correction."

"Correction?" I echoed, the vision flashing vivid before my eyes.

"It means, Elara," Kaeden met my gaze with leaden weight, "they intend to bind your Spark. Irrevocably. To a shard of the Heart of Shadow itself. It'll let them seize total control of your power. And purge it of 'unwanted' elements. Like your own will. Your soul."

Icy horror engulfed me. To become a puppet, soulless and compliant? "No... No! It can't be!"

"Morven convinced the Overlord it's the only way," Kaeden continued, his voice flat, lifeless. "The ritual is set for tomorrow night, at the blood moon's zenith."

"Tomorrow..." I could scarcely breathe. "But... you won't let them? You have to do something!" I searched his face with desperate hope.

"I serve the Overlord," he said slowly. "His command is law."

Hope guttered out. What had I expected, fool that I was? "But..." He looked at me again, and in his eyes blazed a manic fire. "The order was to prepare you. And I will, Elara. But... not as they anticipate."

"What do you mean?"

"They see you as an empty vessel," Kaeden said, drawing closer with predatory intent. "They underestimate you. And the nature of the Life-Giving Spark. It can't simply be bound. It submits willingly—or destroys everything in its path." He halted a pace away. "We have one night, Elara. You mustn't just control your Spark. You must *become* it. Utterly."

"But how? The amulet... it strangles it..."

"Forget the amulet. It doesn't only suppress—it can amplify your power tenfold. If you know how. If you find the key." I stared, breath held. "Tonight, we don't sleep," he said, feverish light in his eyes. "I'll show you what I've shown no one. And you'll either shatter... or become stronger than they could ever imagine."

Fear warred with wild hope within me. This was our sole chance. "I'm... ready," I said.

He led me to the training chamber. But this time, he carried an ebony lacquer box. Unlatching it, he revealed crystals, a bowl of dark, pungent liquid, and a slender silver stylus. "Sit in the center. And remove the amulet," he commanded.

I complied. My Spark flared painfully, flooding me with raw energy. "Now I'll raise a protective circle," Kaeden said, dipping the stylus into the liquid and tracing intricate symbols on the floor. They ignited in ethereal blue light. "It'll contain your power, help you focus it inward."

With the circle sealed, he spoke: "Now, Elara, listen. Immerse in your Spark. Don't just feel it—*become* it. Imagine yourself as pure, radiant light."

I closed my eyes and tried. Thoughts of the ritual, Illiriy, Morven shattered my focus. "Cast it all aside!" Kaeden's voice cracked like a whip. "Nothing exists but you and your Spark! Become it, Elara! Now!"

Again and again, with a doomed woman's desperation, I delved inward. Gradually... it worked. The Spark's warmth swelled, filling me, banishing fear. "Good," Kaeden whispered. "Now... touch the amulet. With your Spark. It's not just your prison. It can be your key."

Mentally, I extended a beam of energy toward the amulet, which Kaeden held near the circle's edge. And felt a response. Cold, but not hostile. "It awaits your command," his voice came again. "It can block—or enhance. Prove you're mistress of your power."

Suddenly, the floor symbols blazed with blinding light. An invisible wall of magic compressed around me, channeling my entire Spark into the amulet. The stone in Kaeden's hand thrummed and ignited with brilliant golden radiance—the light of my Spark.

"Yes! It's working!" Kaeden exhaled in triumph. But in that instant, I sensed something else stirring in the citadel's depths. Something vast, ancient, primordial. And it... it had noticed me.

The door burst open with a thunderous crash. On the threshold, as if birthed from the abyss, loomed a tall figure wreathed in writing shadows, from whose depths two cold, merciless, starlit eyes fixed upon us.

The Overlord.

Chapter 16: Dance
of Fire and Shadow

The Overlord's shadowed form filled the doorway, his inhuman presence crashing over us like a glacial storm bearing death's promise. His eyes—sparkling voids of cosmic chill—pierced first Kaeden's rigid stance, then fixed on me with ravenous hunger. The amulet at my throat, moments ago ablaze, went dark. But my awakened, amplified power still thrummed fiercely within, a caged tempest.

"What an... intriguing surge of energy, Lord Kaeden," the Overlord said, his voice deceptively serene, edged with steel. "I don't recall granting permission for such unauthorized experiments. Especially with a resource so... valuable."

Kaeden straightened in one fluid motion, positioning himself between me and the threat. "My Overlord," he replied, his tone unyielding, devoid of servility. "I was merely accelerating her training. Her power is volatile. I deemed decisive action necessary."

"You *deemed* it necessary?" The Overlord glided into the chamber, his robes whispering soundlessly across the floor. The air thickened, turning frigid. "Curious, when did you begin deciding necessities? Particularly regarding such a prized asset."

"My apologies, my Overlord," Kaeden inclined his head, but his words carried cool, defiant courtesy. "I was merely fulfilling your command."

"Preparing her?" The Overlord uttered a soft, soundless chuckle, more terrifying than any scream. "Or attempting to tame what lies beyond your grasp? To fashion her into your personal blade?" His voice hardened to iron. "I sense her Spark. It's changed. Grown stronger. And far more defiant." He turned to me. "Approach, child. Don't fear. I won't harm you. Not yet."

I froze. Kaeden, ahead of me, gave the subtlest shake of his head. Defiance meant death. Trembling, I stepped forward, wedged between them. "Do you fear me, Elara?" the Overlord asked with honeyed menace that raised the hairs on my neck.

"Yes, my Overlord," I whispered.

"Good. Fear serves a purpose." He drew nearer. I felt an arctic chill and the faint, poisonous perfume of night-blooming flowers. "Morven and Illiriy informed me of the Purification ritual. They believe it's the only way to render your Spark useful. What say you, child? Are you ready to serve me? To offer your gift for Nocturne's glory?"

I flicked a desperate glance at Kaeden, but he was powerless to aid me. I stood alone. "I... I don't know, my Overlord," I forced out. "I'm only beginning to understand my power..."

"Ignorance is no excuse," he cut in coldly. "But perhaps the ritual is premature. If you truly harbor the potential Lord Kaeden so desperately seeks to awaken... or conceal..." His eyes glinted dangerously. "Then we must test it. Immediately. Here and now."

He raised a hand, and motes of concentrated shadow danced at his fingertips. "I wish to witness your raw, primal force. Unleash it. All of it. Now."

"My Overlord, I beg you—this is too perilous!" Kaeden burst out in desperation. "It could kill her!"

"Silence, Lord Kaeden!" The Overlord's voice lashed like a whip. "I'll decide what's perilous. You'll stand and observe."

He regarded me with menace. "Come now, child. Don't keep me waiting. Or must I... assist?"

The shadow motes writhed like venomous serpents. Panic seized me. I knew refusal would mean him ripping the Spark from me by force. I cast a frantic look at Kaeden. He mouthed, "Trust... yourself..." and nodded.

I understood. This was the crux. The choice. Shatter or stake everything.

I closed my eyes, shoving fear aside. I focused on my Spark. Recalled the Star Heart's soaring freedom, the volcanic fury of Kaeden at the Black Lake, his words: *You are the light.*

And I let that light erupt.

It was cataclysmic. A blinding, all-consuming torrent of pure primal energy exploded from me, scouring everything in its path. The protective circle's symbols ignited and crumbled to dust. The amulet seared white-hot at my throat, then shattered with a crystalline chime. I saw nothing but searing brilliance. Heard nothing but the roar of this power. I *was* it. I was the storm.

Then it ceased.

I stood amid the chamber, gasping. The light faded, leaving hollow exhaustion and impossible lightness. I was unbound.

I opened my eyes. The Overlord remained in place, but his icy composure had fractured. His eyes widened in astonishment, mingled with... disbelief? Or was it fear? Faint smoke curled from his dark robes.

Lord Kaeden stood apart, shielding his face with one hand. But through his fingers, I glimpsed the convulsive gleam in his eyes—shock, relief, and... pride?

The doors crashed open, and Morven and Illiriy burst in, faces etched with alarm. "My Overlord! What transpired here?!" they cried. "We sensed an unprecedented magical surge!"

The Overlord lowered his hand slowly. He studied me with a long, probing gaze. Then he smiled. A genuine, broad, almost childlike smile that transformed his features, rendering him even more unearthly beautiful—and utterly terrifying.

"What transpired is what I've awaited so long," he said, his voice ringing with mad triumph. "A true awakening. It seems our stubborn Lord Kaeden was right. She is the one we need."

He looked at me again. "The ritual is canceled. It's obsolete. I have far more... intriguing plans for you, Elara."

With regal poise, he extended his pale, elegant hand. "Approach, child. Fear me no longer. Your true training begins now. And henceforth, your sole mentor... shall be me."

Chapter 17: In the Overlord's Chambers

The Overlord's words—"your mentor... shall be me"—struck like a fate worse than any sentence. I stood frozen until, with a light yet imperious gesture, he beckoned me to follow. "Come, Elara. We have much to accomplish. And precious little time, if we're to save this world from itself."

Kaeden, rigid and ashen, tensed sharply. I saw the manic fire ignite in his eyes. He wanted to speak, but held his tongue. He merely watched in silent, excruciating despair as the Overlord laid his chill fingers on my shoulder and guided me toward the exit. As we passed, I stole a glance at Kaeden. In his gaze burned helpless fury, pain... and desperate concern. For me?

Morven and Illiriy bowed obsequiously. In Illiriy's venomous eyes, I glimpsed bitter disappointment and envy. Their schemes for me had crumbled. Now, I was the personal "property" of the Overlord himself.

They didn't return me to my cell. The Overlord led me through a procession of opulent, foreboding halls. Walls of black marble bore ancient artifacts, each radiating an oppressive magical aura. I glimpsed ornate weapons, weathered scrolls, and throbbing crystals.

At last, we paused before towering doors of ebony wood. "These will be your new quarters," the Overlord said with a smile that chilled me. "While you're under my... special patronage."

The doors parted silently. The chamber was immense. A bed of extravagant size draped in a dark violet velvet canopy, embroidered with silver stars. An elegant writing desk, shelves crammed with ancient tomes. Plush rugs carpeted the floor. And even... a real window, unbarred. It overlooked Nocturne itself, sprawling in a colossal subterranean cavern. The city of shadows pulsed with its enigmatic, terrifying, and mesmerizing life.

"I think you'll find it to your liking," the Overlord murmured, his voice brushing my ear. He carried the scent of ozone and unfamiliar, wintry blooms. "Here, you'll sense Nocturne's true grandeur. And your new place within it."

"What place is that... in this grandeur?" I whispered.

"You are my key, child. My most coveted key," he said, resting an icy hand on my shoulder with deceptive gentleness. "The key to Etheria's future. A future without the Gloom Blight. Only perfect order. *My* order."

He guided me to an ornate chair, throne-like in its grace. "Your training begins at once. Sit." I obeyed, feeling like a mouse before a serpent. "Lord Kaeden taught you crude control. Morven immersed you in esoteric theories. Both too primitive," the Overlord paced slowly. "Your Spark isn't mere energy. It's the pure echo of creation itself. It can be not just controlled—but shaped. Harnessed for grand creation... or utter devastation."

He raised a hand, and a sphere of blinding white light bloomed in his palm. "That's... light," I stammered.

"Yes, child," he smiled indulgently. "I too can wield light. Your Spark is an uncut diamond. It requires expert faceting to become a treasure. Or the deadliest weapon."

With a snap of his fingers, the orb morphed into a tiny bird that fluttered from his hand and alighted on my shoulder, bestowing gentle warmth. "Magic is will," the Overlord continued. "You must learn to command your Spark. Bend it to your desires. To work miracles... or deliver death." The light-bird dissolved into a cascade of golden motes.

"Now you," he said. "Focus. Imagine a flower. But don't revive a withered stem. Create one anew. From pure light."

I closed my eyes, willing fear away. It felt impossible. Yet his unshakeable conviction infected me with fragile belief. I attuned to my Spark. Unfettered by the amulet, it pulsed like a miniature sun within. I envisioned a simple field bloom with azure petals. I poured my will into the image.

I felt the Spark gather in my palms. Opening my eyes, I beheld it: a flower, small and imperfect, but real. It glowed with soft, vital warmth. It lived.

"Not bad... for a first attempt," the Overlord said, satisfaction threading his voice. "You possess a rare gift. It seems Lord Kaeden laid a solid foundation after all." I gazed at the luminous bloom, tears pricking my eyes. My own small miracle.

"But this is merely the beginning," he grew solemn. "Your Spark can achieve more. It can mend wounds inflicted by the Gloom Blight. Restore life to scorched earth. And..." His gaze sharpened to predatory keenness. "...mercilessly eradicate those who defy my will. If properly directed."

He moved to the window. "This world is dying, Elara. In its death throes. I'm striving to salvage what's possible. To forge a new order from the ruins. But I need power. *Your* power." He whirled back, eyes ablaze with fanatic zeal. "Will you help me save Etheria? Surrender your Spark, your will to me? Even if it means wielding your gift in ways you never imagined? Even if it requires you to become... something greater than human?"

His words were so persuasive, so alluring. To save Etheria...
Wasn't that my dream? But at what cost? And could I trust
him—this being forged from shadow itself?

The glowing flower in my hands began to wilt, petal by
petal.

I didn't know how to answer. But one truth anchored me:
my true path in Nocturne had only just begun. And it would
prove far more labyrinthine and perilous than I could ever
have dreamed.

Chapter 18: Art of Darkness, Art of Light

The days following the observatory lesson blurred into a relentless cycle of grueling training and shattering revelations. The Overlord bore no resemblance to my prior mentors. Kaeden had sought to forge my Spark in the vise of discipline; Morven, to lure it into the mists of arcane knowledge. The Overlord, however, aimed not to restrain my power—but to unleash it. Utterly. Then tame it, bend it, direct it wherever he deemed fit. To craft me into his most exquisite weapon.

Our "lessons" unfolded across the citadel's varied realms. Sometimes in his opulent yet frigid chambers, where he compelled me to meditate for hours, shaping my Spark's light into ever more intricate constructs: not just blooms, but paradise birds in flight, snarling shadow wolves, gleaming blades of radiance. "Your Spark," he intoned in that hypnotic timbre, "is the extension of your will. Whatever you truly believe, you can manifest."

At other times, he led me into the shadowed underbelly, where the Gloom Blight's venomous breath pressed tangibly against the skin. There, he forced me to mend the ravaged earth. It was torment. I felt my power clash with the darkness, even as the Blight clawed to corrupt my light. Several times, I teetered on madness's edge, saved only by the Overlord's imperious intervention—his dark aura enveloping me like a protective shroud. "You must learn to walk the precipice," he'd say afterward, as I lay spent on the chill stone. "Only there, on the boundary of light and shadow, will you grasp your Spark's true potency."

He was a devilish manipulator, attuned to my fears and wielding them without mercy. He played upon my ambitions, murmuring promises of grand destiny. With mesmerizing eloquence, he painted his vision of Etheria's future—a realm of flawless order. And in those moments, listening to him, I began to believe. But then I'd recall the glacial chill emanating from him, and realize his "perfect order" would rise upon the bones of any who dared defy it.

Under his guidance, my Spark burgeoned daily. I mastered elaborate light-forms, discerned magical currents, perceived auras. But at what price? I sensed his influence deepening, his philosophy seeping into my thoughts, warping my worldview.

Interactions with Nocturne's other denizens dwindled to nothing. Servants averted their eyes in terror. As the Overlord's "personal pupil," I was more isolated than ever.

I heard nothing of Kaeden. Had he been punished? Exiled? I thought of him often. And the more I learned of the Overlord, the more complex my feelings toward Kaeden grew. He was cruel, yes—but his cruelty held a stark, unyielding honesty. He never sought to deceive me. In him burned far more life, more humanity, than in the luminous yet hollow Overlord.

One day, I crossed paths with Morven. "Child of the Spark," his violet eyes appraised me keenly. "I see your training advances with startling speed." A veiled bitterness laced his voice—perhaps even envy. "But remember, Elara: true power lies in profound understanding. Let no one blind you. Seek truth within yourself. And in the silence."

He vanished, leaving me adrift in fresh uncertainties.

One evening, as I labored—exhausted—to weave a luminous star-map from my Spark, the Overlord declared, "You are ready, Elara." I looked up in alarm. "Ready? For what?"

"For your first true trial. The purpose of your training." He gestured toward the cavern's distant egress. "Beyond the Shadow Fangs lies a place wholly consumed by the Blight. An ancient, sacred forest. No mortal can enter. None. Except you."

My heart stuttered in dread. "You... want me to go there? Alone?"

"Not merely go. You must heal it. Restore its life. Your Spark alone can achieve this. It will be your inaugural triumph over Shadow. Proof that you are the key I've sought so long."

To mend a dead, cursed wood? It felt like sanctioned suicide. "But... I'm not sure I can..."

"You will," his voice brooked no doubt. "You have no choice. And because—" A chilling smile curved his lips. "—this time, I go with you. I'll oversee your victory personally."

He'd accompany me? The notion horrified even as it offered faint solace. "At dawn tomorrow, we depart for the Darkwood," he proclaimed. "Rest now. You'll need every shred of strength."

He departed. I remained alone, facing the gravest ordeal of my life. For the first time, fear mingled not just with terror, but with a sharp, anticipatory ache. I was becoming a weapon. But whose? And against what true foe would my awakened power ultimately turn?

Chapter 19: Heart of Darkness, Heart of Light

Dawn over Nocturne was a surreal spectacle. Sickly crimson and indigo lights faded slowly into a spectral gray pallor. They roused me long before. Two silent maids delivered sturdy garb of dark leather and a travel pack with water and hardtack.

The Overlord awaited at the egress. He wore simple traveling attire of impeccably tanned black hide and a long hooded cloak that veiled his features. Flanking him were two of his personal sentinels—ashen-skinned beings with inhuman violet eyes. "Ready, child?" His even voice thrummed with impatience and predatory anticipation. I nodded mutely. Choice was a luxury I no longer possessed.

We departed Nocturne via a hidden tunnel. Emerging topside, I squinted against the daylight. The air was crisp, scented with earth and recent rain. But as we pressed on, the Gloom Blight's festering presence intensified. The ground turned ashen, fissured like parched skin. Trees loomed as blackened, twisted skeletons. The atmosphere grew leaden, laced with the nauseating tang of decay.

The Overlord strode ahead, his cloak billowing like a raptor's wings. His guards glided at our flanks, ghostly and silent. I followed, heart pounding with dread.

"This is the Darkwood, Elara," the Overlord intoned as we neared the fringe of the vast, necrotic forest. "Once the most exquisite and sacred wood in all Etheria. The Heart of the World. And now…" With concealed anguish, he swept a hand over the barren expanse. "…merely a breeding ground for the Gloom Blight. A rotting wound upon this realm."

I gazed into the horrific thicket, primal terror coiling in my gut. Tree trunks bore repulsive, throbbing growths. Branches wove an impenetrable canopy. The soil squelched underfoot, exhaling toxic vapors. Silence reigned—absolute, lifeless.

"Your task, Elara," the Overlord turned to me, "is to enter this forest and cleanse it. Restore its vitality. Begin modestly. Select a small patch. Focus. And wield your Spark."

"But… how?" I whispered. "It's so… immense. Hopeless."

"Greatness sprouts from the small," he said, placing an icy hand on my shoulder. "Fear not. I'll stand with you. Recall what I've taught."

He led me to a scrap of ground where faint grass remnants lingered. I drew a deep breath, shut my eyes, and attuned to my Spark. I envisioned that patch verdant with emerald blades and delicate blooms. I channeled my light, meeting the Blight's ferocious resistance—cold, cloying, malevolent. Gritting my teeth, I poured forth with desperate fervor.

At last, I opened my eyes. Where barren soil had been, a verdant islet now thrived. And at its center bloomed a solitary azure flower. "Not bad," the Overlord murmured softly. "Very not bad. You see? You *can* reclaim life."

I stared at the fragile bloom, tears welling—born of exhaustion… and pride. I had done it.

But my elation was fleeting. A chorus of bone-chilling howls echoed from the depths. "They've sensed you, child," the Overlord tensed, his hand drifting to the hilt of a sword that materialized from thin air. "Sensed your light. The Tainted. And there are many."

Dark silhouettes emerged from the trees. Enormous, wolf-like horrors—larger and fiercer than any before, eyes blazing crimson. At least a dozen. The guards thrust forth wands of black metal, which ignited in violet luminescence, erecting a shimmering barrier. "Defend yourself, Elara!" the Overlord commanded. "Harness your Spark! Don't let them breach!"

The Tainted lunged with savage snarls. The shield crackled, fissures spiderwebbing its surface. I stood paralyzed by fear. "Don't falter!" The Overlord's voice cracked like a lash. "You are light! They are wretched shadow! Burn them!"

I squeezed my eyes shut, summoning my Spark. This time, I conjured not a flower, but a searing, annihilating beam lancing from my palms. I directed it at a colossal Tainted battering the barrier.

The ray struck its chest. A harrowing shriek rent the air as the beast ignited, crumbling to a vortex of black ash. The magical shield shattered with a resonant snap. The remaining horde surged with redoubled fury.

The guards engaged, their arms morphing into violet light-blades. The Overlord's sword blurred in inhuman arcs. And I... I staggered, drained, firing desperate light-bolts to aid them. Each strike throbbed dully within me, but I persisted.

The skirmish was brief and brutal. As the last Tainted collapsed, I dropped to my knees, utterly spent. The Overlord casually wiped his blade and approached. "You fought, child. Far better than I anticipated." He extended a peremptory hand. "Rise. This is merely the prelude. The Darkwood yields nothing easily."

I regarded my trembling hand. Then him—his towering shadowed form, his glacial eyes. And with horrifying clarity, I knew he spoke true. This was only the beginning. My path through the darkness had grown infinitely more treacherous. More... futile.

Chapter 20: Lament
of the Dead Forest

I collapsed onto the ground, gasping for breath. My hands trembled, my mind buzzed with exhaustion. The fight had been brief, but draining. Each flare of my Spark stole a fragment of me, leaving a hollow ache in its wake.

The Overlord approached soundlessly and offered a flask of water. His ashen-skinned guards, unscathed, inspected the heaps of black ash from our fallen foes. "You've surpassed my expectations, Elara," he said evenly, though a note of surprise colored his tone. "Your Spark wields not only creation, but formidable destruction. That's promising."

"Promising?" I lifted my gaze to him with effort. "I killed them. They were once alive... That's not what my power is meant for."

"In this world, child, creation sometimes demands ruthless destruction," he replied, a condescending smirk in his voice. "To heal a festering wound, one must excise the rot. Remember that." He helped me to my feet. "Now rest. We have a long road ahead."

We made camp. I leaned against a tree trunk, while the Overlord stood apart, gazing into the thicket. "Why this forest?" I couldn't hold back.

"Because the Darkwood is no mere woodland," he said quietly, and in his voice, I caught echoes of something human.

"It's a symbol. Once the heart of Etheria. If we can heal it, it will kindle hope across the realm. It will prove the Blight can be vanquished." He paused. "And it will be... my personal triumph. Over the past. Over mistakes. Over... myself." The final words carried such profound anguish that my heart clenched.

Soon, we pressed on, delving into the cursed forest's core. The trees grew more grotesque, their trunks oozing black mold. Beneath our feet squelched viscous mire, reeking of putrefaction. We advanced through perpetual, oppressive gloom. The woods pressed not just physically, but spiritually. I heard faint whispers, murmuring my fears, the futility of our quest.

The Overlord seemed oblivious. Only occasionally did he halt, commanding me to cleanse another patch—a stream, a withered tree, a glade blanketed in slimy fungi.

Each effort sapped me utterly. The Blight resisted with savage, almost sentient fury. But I endured. I recalled Kaeden's lessons on control, the soaring unity at the Star Heart. And I fought. Sometimes, when I thought I could bear no more, success came. I'd watch the black mold recede, a stream run clear, a single green shoot pierce dead bark. These small victories fueled me onward.

The Overlord observed intently, intervening rarely—offering terse, precise guidance: "Focus on the Blight's source." "Don't scatter your power." "Wield not just light, but will. *Command* the Blight to yield."

Once, while purifying a forest pond, I felt not mere resistance, but a profound, unbearable sorrow emanating from the lifeless soil itself. "You're beginning to sense it," the Overlord said when I told him, a melancholic note in his voice. "This forest isn't simply dead. It suffers. The Blight doesn't just kill—it torments. Perhaps your Spark can heal not only its form... but touch its anguished soul."

Days blurred. Nights were frigid, rife with ominous sounds. The Overlord required no rest. Often, he'd vanish into the shadows, as if attuned to whispers beyond my ken.

One morning, we emerged onto a vast clearing. At its center loomed a colossal, ancient tree—or what remained of it. Its mighty trunk, riven by lightning, was marred by black, pulsating sores that wept concentrated darkness. Waves of primal, devouring Blight radiated from it. "There it is," the Overlord whispered. "The Heart of the Darkwood. The core of the Gloom Blight in this forest."

I stared at the monstrous growth, horror flooding me. It wasn't merely dead. It was malevolent. I felt it reach for my Spark, hungering to consume.

"You must heal it, Elara," the Overlord turned to me, his eyes alight with desperate resolve. "Only you can. This is our sole chance. But it will be... deadly perilous."

Abruptly, a tall, skeletal figure rose from the tree's roots, clad in tattered rags. Its eyes glowed with dim, marsh-fire luminescence. "Who dares disturb the Master of this Forest's repose?" rasped a voice like splintering, rotting timber.

"We come to free this wood," the Overlord stepped forward. "It has suffered too long under your dominion, Twisted Spirit of the Ancient Tree."

The spirit emitted a venomous, hissing laugh. "Free? Fools. This forest is mine. And you..." Its boggy eyes fixed on me. "...you reek of life. Such irritating light. My woods will not abide it."

It slammed its staff into the earth. The ground quaked. Twisted black roots, sharp as steel spears, erupted from the soil, writhing like colossal serpents—and lunged straight for us.

Chapter 21: Gift
of the Ancient Heart

The Twisted Spirit howled in fury, swinging its staff with savage force. The earth shuddered. Jagged black roots, writhing like ravenous serpents, surged toward us. "Protect her!" The Overlord's voice boomed like thunder.

His two guards advanced, their wands igniting in violet radiance to form a flickering barrier. The roots slammed against it with a deafening crack, but the shield held. I saw the sentinels' forms strain under the assault.

The Overlord blurred forward in impossible speed, his sword carving a lethal arc that severed several tendrils. Black, foul ichor sprayed from the wounds. "Elara!" he shouted, his deadly dance unbroken. "The tree! Your target is the Forest's Heart! Heal it, or we're all lost here!"

I stood stunned. But his desperate command snapped me from paralysis. The tree. Our only hope. Yet chaos swirled: the battle raged, and from the woods' depths slunk more Tainted beasts, grotesque and ferocious beyond reckoning.

I squeezed my eyes shut, banishing fear to summon my Spark. I envisioned the Forest's Heart as it ought to be—towering, radiant, verdant. Arms extended, I channeled my full will toward the dying colossus. A torrent of golden light erupted from my palms. But the Spirit yielded nothing. A viscous black surge lashed back, meeting my glow.

The forces collided in a deafening rupture. The backlash hurled me rearward. My Spark faltered against the onslaught of malice. "Don't yield, child!" the Overlord roared. "It feeds on your fear! Show it your light's might!"

His words ignited fresh resolve. I surged my Spark anew, infusing it with all my anguish for this tormented wood, all my rage. My light blazed brighter, fiercer. It inched through the shadow's veil.

The Twisted Spirit wailed in agony and wrath, unleashing another wave of darkness at me. I countered with my radiance—and for an instant, behind the mask of hatred, glimpsed its true essence. Once a wise guardian of these woods, twisted by the Blight into a suffering abomination. "It... it's in pain," I whispered.

"Compassion is your fatal flaw!" the Overlord bellowed. "Destroy it, or it'll slaughter us without mercy!"

But I couldn't. I directed my Spark at the Spirit—not to annihilate, but to embrace with gentle warmth. I sought the flicker of light that might yet linger within. The figure stilled. In its eyes flashed astonishment. Anguish. Hope?

In that frozen heartbeat, the Overlord seized the opening. His sword, wreathed in ebony flame, plunged through the Spirit's form.

It uttered a final, prolonged, almost human moan and dissolved into dust.

With that, the energy shrouding the Darkwood's Heart quivered and receded. The trunk's sores began to knit. And from a barren limb sprouted a single, delicate green shoot.

My strength ebbed utterly. My legs buckled, and I sank toward the earth. Strong arms caught me—the Overlord's. His face was pallid, but his eyes blazed with manic triumph.

"You've done it, Elara," he murmured. "You've healed it. You've won. You truly are the key."

I gazed at the transformed tree. Around us, the forest stirred. Shadows retreated; the air filled with the scent of fresh soil.

But the ground beneath the Heart trembled once more. From the roots welled a soft, silvery glow. "What is that?" I breathed.

"Ancient, purest magic," the Overlord muttered, genuine awe in his voice. "The Heart... it's not just mending. It's awakening. Granting us its power."

The light flared blindingly. I shielded my eyes. When vision cleared, a massive, luminous seed hovered before me—heart-sized, pulsing with such vital warmth it embodied life's essence itself.

Before the Overlord or I could react, the seed descended... into my outstretched, trembling hands.

It was warm, alive. My Spark resonated, merging with it seamlessly—like two raindrops reunited.

Then... the world dimmed. The last sight was the Overlord's face, etched with shock and disbelief.

Chapter 22: Whisper of the Ancient Heart and the Icy Breath of Nocturne

Consciousness returned in fits and starts. First, I felt an astonishing warmth in my palms, as if cradling a miniature sun, and a dull ache suffusing my body. With effort, I pried my eyes open.

I lay upon the Overlord's unfurled cloak, beneath the canopy of the colossal tree—the Heart of the Darkwood—which now appeared utterly transformed. The blackness had receded, revealing healthy bark aglow with inner golden light. Upon branches that had been barren the day before, thousands of tiny green leaves now budded. The air was pure, scented with damp earth and vitality.

And in my hands, clasped tightly to my chest, rested the glowing seed. It was warm, emanating a gentle vibration that eased my pain, filling me with quiet, luminous joy.

"Awake, child?" I startled. The Overlord sat nearby on a fallen log, watching me intently. His face bore traces of weariness, but his eyes gleamed with a new intensity—a blend of awe, contemplation, and... reverence. His two guards stood motionless at a distance, their violet eyes fixed on the seed in my grasp.

"What... what is it?" I whispered, lifting the seed. It shone with a warm, silvery radiance.

"I don't know, Elara," the Overlord said, shaking his head slowly. "Ancient legends speak of Forest Hearts—seeds that birth new Trees of Life. I dismissed them as fables. It seems I was mistaken." He met my gaze. "It emerged when you healed this tree. When your Spark merged with its soul. It... chose you."

Chose me? I studied the seed again. It seemed fragile yet brimming with inconceivable power. My Spark responded to it with eager kinship, like a long-lost companion calling home.

"First, you must regain your strength," the Overlord said, his tone laced with an odd, paternal solicitude. "You teetered on the brink. Then we'll unravel this gift. And how it might serve Etheria's salvation."

We lingered at the awakened tree's base for several days. To my surprise, the Overlord abandoned his haste. He spent hours in silent observation—of me, of the luminous seed. He even fetched my meals himself: forest berries, roasted game.

The seed, which I'd silently dubbed the Heart of Light, mended me with astonishing speed. My Spark grew stronger, purer, more radiant each day. The surrounding woods transformed apace. Glades greened; birdsong returned. The Gloom Blight withdrew.

"This is your doing, Elara," the Overlord said one evening by the fire. "Your Spark, amplified by the Heart of Light, is healing this land."

"But I'm not doing it deliberately," I confessed. "It simply... happens."

"Sometimes the greatest magic arises intuitively," he mused. "Morven sought to teach you to comprehend magic. Kaeden, to master it. I..." A melancholic note crept into his voice. "...I merely guided you to where your true nature could unfold."

On our final day, he announced abruptly that we must return. "But the forest... it's not fully healed," I protested anxiously.

"You've done enough," his voice hardened once more. "Now the woods must sustain itself. You're needed in Nocturne. This Heart of Light... it could be the key to redeeming all Etheria. And far more. You must learn to wield its power deliberately."

I didn't want to leave, but I knew he was right. The journey back differed profoundly. The revitalized forest bade us farewell with rustling leaves and avian chorus. The Tainted had vanished. I carried the Heart of Light pressed to my chest like an inestimable treasure.

As we reentered Nocturne's somber tunnels, I felt my Spark and the Heart contract in pained recoil. Yet the old terror had ebbed. In its place burned cold resolve—and newfound strength.

At my chambers, a surprise awaited. Leaning against the wall stood Lord Kaeden. Spotting us, his face flickered with emotion before resuming its stoic mask. In his eyes, I caught a flash of desperate relief. "Overlord," he nodded curtly, then his gaze locked on the glowing seed in my hands. "What... is that?"

"This, my loyal Lord Kaeden, is our new advantage," the Overlord smirked. "It seems your former pupil has surprised us all." He turned to me. "Rest, Elara. Tomorrow, we resume our explorations. I already have ideas for... utilizing this."

He departed, leaving me alone with Kaeden. We regarded each other in silence. "Are you... all right?" he asked at last, his voice uncharacteristically soft.

"Yes. I think... yes."

"What is that thing?" He eyed the seed warily. I recounted everything. Kaeden listened, his frown deepening. "Tree of

Life... its seed," he murmured. "I've heard the legends, but never believed... This changes everything, Elara."

"What changes?" I asked, a chill prickling my spine.

"Your role in this war. Your place in the Overlord's designs. And..." His gaze grew weighted. "...mine." He met my eyes, shadowed with grim determination. "The Overlord will stop at nothing for power. If this Heart of Light is as potent as it seems... he'll exploit it. And you. At any cost."

He stepped closer. "Be exceedingly cautious, Elara. I beg you. The Overlord isn't what he pretends. He's ancient, merciless evil. And his true schemes may be far more horrifying than you can imagine."

Before I could reply, he turned sharply and strode away. I stood alone, clutching the radiant Heart of Light. His final, urgent words echoed in my soul: *Be cautious...*

But how does one tread carefully in darkness's very core, when in your hands lies the sole key to a world's salvation—or its doom?

Chapter 23: Games of Shadows
and Shards of Light

Kaeden's icy words—"The Overlord isn't what he seems"—echoed relentlessly in my ears. I returned to my lavish chambers, stumbling from exhaustion. The Heart of Light, resting on the table, cast a gentle glow, but I could no longer regard it with untainted joy. Its radiance felt shadowed now. No longer just a miracle, it was a potential weapon in the Overlord's grasp.

He arrived at my door the next morning. To my dread, Morven accompanied him. In the Keeper of Arcane Lore's eyes, I glimpsed the jealous curiosity of a scholar robbed of a priceless specimen. "Good morning, Child of the Spark," the Overlord said, his voice deceptively mild. "I trust you rested well. Today promises fascinating work. This..." He nodded toward the Heart of Light. "...demands immediate scrutiny. We must uncover its essence, its potentials. And how it binds to you."

Thus began a new, terrifying phase of my "training." Now they collaborated. And I was their lab rat.

For hours, they pored over the Heart, hauling in ancient tomes and arranging peculiar crystals around it. They murmured guttural incantations that chilled my blood. My role was humiliating: at their command, I touched the Heart again and again, channeled my Spark into it, then detailed every

ASTRID LOVELL

sensation. Sometimes the Overlord clasped my hands in his, guiding my power with his unyielding will to awaken the artifact's hidden facets. His touch was frigid, yet it emanated such potency that my breath caught in a tangle of fear and forbidden awe.

The Heart of Light unveiled its secrets piecemeal. It harbored boundless healing: wilted blooms revived at its mere brush. It could forge impenetrable wards. And it... possessed a mind of its own. In moments of contact, vivid, fragmented visions assailed me: emerald groves, gleaming metropolises, forgotten eras when the world was young. "It holds this realm's memory," the Overlord declared, eyes alight with triumph. "Memories of Etheria before Shadow's fall. And within lies the key to its rebirth."

Morven fixated on the Heart's resonance with magical flows. "This relic," he intoned in his hypnotic cadence, "acts as a tuning fork, amplifying any arcane energies. Master it, and we could reshape reality's weave itself." His words sent shivers racing down my spine.

I saw nothing of Kaeden. He had been deliberately sidelined, and it gnawed at me. His desperate warning—"Don't trust"—resounded in my mind with every syllable from the Overlord.

The Overlord relished his mentor's mantle. He proved surprisingly patient, elucidating arcane complexities. Yet beneath his paternal warmth lurked glacial calculation. I was but a tool.

One day, he escorted me to Nocturne's lower depths. In a dimly lit hall stood endless ranks of warriors. Their ebony armor etched with runes pulsing crimson, beneath helmets swirled only roiling void. "These are my Silent Sentinels," the Overlord said with pride. "Perfected soldiers, unknowing of fear or pain. But their vigor draws from a dark font, alas, vulnerable to the Blight's taint."

He led me to one. From the Sentinel emanated chill and a muffled, excruciating agony—as if, within that shell, some warped soul still writhed. "Your Spark, bolstered by the Heart of Light," the Overlord said, his gaze predatory, "can purge what the darkest sorcery has twisted. Try, child. Touch it. Let your light pierce this abyss."

I stared at him in horror. Purify *this*? A being of pure shadow? Trembling, I extended a hand to the cold plate. Summoning all my resolve, I invoked my Spark. At first, nothing stirred. Then... a faint response. Not from the armor, but from the darkness's core. A spark of life. Instinctively, I poured my full radiance toward it.

In that instant, a vision seized me: a young, fair-haired warrior, battling fiercely for his convictions... then engulfing shadow, unbearable torment, eternal despair. When I blinked back to reality, tears streamed down my face. The Sentinel stood unmoving. But for a fleeting moment, its runes had flickered not crimson, but pure, golden light.

"Intriguing," the Overlord murmured thoughtfully. "Very intriguing. It seems your gifts are even more multifaceted than I dared hope." I realized: this was a fresh, more harrowing trial.

That evening, drained and solitary, I heard a faint rustle at the door. I froze. No servant this. Someone furtively slid something beneath. On the shadowed floor appeared a small, tightly folded scrap of parchment.

With shaking hands, I unfolded it. In a familiar, angular script were scrawled just two words: *Don't trust.* And beneath, a signature I'd recognize amid thousands. Kaeden.

Chapter 24: Note in the Dark

Kaeden's note—that tiny scrap of parchment—burned in my palm like a live coal. *Don't trust.* Two words encapsulating a universe of doubt, peril, and elusive hope. Whom not to trust? The Overlord? The answer seemed plain. But what if this was yet another, more cunning snare? Could I rely on Kaeden, my abductor, servant of shadows?

I hid the note beneath my mattress, feeling like a conspirator in some forbidden intrigue. Every rustle beyond the door now heralded exposure.

My "lessons" with the Overlord persisted, but I attended them with redoubled wariness. His philosophy of cosmic order, his impassioned tales of Etheria's redemption—all now filtered through suspicion's lens. I desperately sought the undercurrents in his speeches: true motives, deceptions. And the more I probed, the more I unearthed. His "noble" ends forever justified ruthless means. His "perfect order" demanded slavish obedience. His "bright future" was steeped in Nocturne's ominous hues.

The experiments with the Silent Sentinels devolved into moral agony. The Overlord obsessed over "purifying" them via my Spark and the Heart of Light. Each touch of their frigid armor summoned flashes of their pasts—vibrant lives cruelly stolen, luminous souls enslaved by darkness. I wasn't certain my "cleansing" brought relief. It felt as if I only amplified their torment.

"You're doubting again, child?" The Overlord, with his preternatural insight, always detected my inner turmoil. "Doubt is poison, Elara. It erodes your will. You must believe. Blindly. Unquestioningly." But I couldn't. Kaeden's note had planted the very seed of skepticism he dreaded.

I scrutinized the tomes he provided with fierce intensity, hunting inconsistencies, veiled meanings. In one ancient chronicle, I stumbled upon references to the "Light Devourers"—potent entities capable of absorbing pure magic to augment their shadowed might. The descriptions were nebulous, yet something in them chilled me to the core. Could the Overlord be one? Was that why he craved my Spark so?

I yearned to contact Kaeden, but it was impossible. My chambers were guarded more vigilantly than ever.

One day, the Overlord led me to a vast subterranean chamber that proved... a conservatory. Beneath the glow of arcane crystals flourished fantastical flora: luminous mosses, colossal blooms, trees with silver foliage. The place was achingly beautiful, yet utterly unnatural. Too pristine. "My private garden," the Overlord said. "Here, I've gathered Etheria's rarest, most exquisite remnants." He guided me to a pool where enormous white lilies drifted. "Even flawless beauty requires sustenance, child. As does your Spark."

He took my hand, drawing it toward a lily. "Share your power. Make it shine brighter." I funneled a sliver of my Spark into the bloom. It did gleam more vividly. But in tandem, I felt something drain from me. Not mere energy. A fragment of my light. My very soul.

"See, child?" The Overlord smiled with satisfaction. "To gain, one must give." Venomous deceit lurked in his words once more. I yanked my hand back. "And what do *you* give, my Overlord?" I challenged.

"Everything," he replied softly, a inhuman weariness threading his tone. "My life. My immortality. All for this dying Etheria's salvation. All for the order I must impose." I didn't believe him. Not for an instant.

That evening, desperation hardened into resolve. I *had* to uncover the truth. Reach Kaeden again. I recalled the Silent Sentinels. If my Spark could touch whatever remnant of life lingered within... perhaps one might carry a message.

It was a mad, suicidal scheme. But it was all I had.

The next day, as the Overlord brought me back to the Sentinels' hall, I knew my course. I selected an unassuming one in the rear ranks. He ordered me to "purify" it. Approaching, I feigned channeling my Spark while desperately sending a silent, mental plea. With all my might, I projected the call.

And suddenly... a faint but unmistakable response. Subtle as a zephyr's whisper. The Sentinel's runes flickered—not crimson, but pure golden light, if only for a breath.

"Enough," the Overlord's voice cut in, cold and curt, halting my efforts. "You're unusually distracted today." He seemed disappointed. Evidently, he'd noticed nothing amiss. As we departed, I cast a final glance at *my* Sentinel. It stood inert. But I knew. It had heard.

That night, I retrieved my sole scrap of parchment. I scrawled one word: *Where?* Beneath it, I sketched the sigil of the Light's Guardians.

The following day, while "purifying" the same Sentinel, I slipped the note unseen beneath a armor plate on its arm. My heart thundered. If the Overlord spotted it... it would be my end. But he didn't. And *my* Sentinel remained as mute as ever. I had no idea if my desperate gambit would succeed. But it was my only, final tether to hope. And I clung to it fiercely.

Chapter 25: Thread
of Light in the Darkness

The days after my desperate bid to pass the note stretched into a torment of anticipation. Every whisper of sound made me flinch. Each morning, en route to the Silent Sentinels' hall, I stole furtive glances at *my* warrior, straining for any sign. But he remained as immobile as ever.

The Overlord approved of my feigned diligence. The experiments with my Spark and the Heart of Light grew ever more intricate—and perilous. He compelled me to channel energy streams across vast distances, to sense and categorize Nocturne's magical currents, to erect light-barriers that he tested with his own assaults. Each "lesson" left me hollowed out, but I clenched my jaw and endured. Now I had purpose: await Kaeden's reply.

I listened to the Overlord with heightened vigilance, sifting truth from deception. He spoke eloquently of Etheria's grand future, his voice laced with such fanatical conviction that, at times, I succumbed to his shadowy allure. But then I'd recall the chill in his eyes, his ruthlessness—and Kaeden's note: *Don't trust.* All his eloquent promises crumbled to dust.

Morven, too, paid me undue attention. He appeared at several "lessons," posing insidious questions about magic's nature, my sensations, my dreams. I answered evasively, sensing his suspicion.

One day, as I "worked" with *my* Sentinel once more, I felt it again. A feather-light brush against my hand. I jerked back in fright, heart racing. But touching again yielded nothing. Had I imagined it?

The next day, approaching the Sentinel, I was prepared. I sent my most fervent mental summons. As my hand met its armor, the subtle pressure returned. And from the corner of my eye, I spotted a tiny edge of grayish parchment peeking from beneath a plate.

My heart leaped with joy—and seized in terror. A response. He'd answered!

I glanced about in panic. The Overlord stood at the hall's far end, conferring with Magister Illiriy. They paid me no heed.

With trembling fingers, I deftly hooked the parchment and withdrew it in one swift motion. I slipped the small, tightly rolled note into a hidden pocket. The remainder of the "lesson" passed in agony, every moment an eternity.

At last, the ordeal ended. The instant my chamber door sealed, I rushed to the table, extracting the precious missive. It was briefer than mine. A few words in that familiar, angular script: *Library. Tonight. Midnight. South Archive. Carefully. Not alone.*

The library? Midnight? And *Not alone.* Would he bring an ally? Or was this a warning of some fresh trap?

I'd go. No matter what. This was my sole chance.

But how to escape? The magical seal on the door was impenetrable. In desperation, I approached the window. It overlooked a sheer wall plummeting hundreds of meters into abyss. I reread the note. Then gazed at the Heart of Light glowing on the table. Inspiration struck.

The Overlord himself had handed me the key to freedom. He'd taught me to shape light into complex forms. What if I could craft something sturdier? More utilitarian?

It was folly. But I had to try.

I sank to the floor, placing the Heart of Light before me. Eyes closed, I focused. Not a fragile bloom this time, but a rope. Long, impossibly resilient, woven from condensed light. I channeled my Spark into the vision, amplified by the Heart's radiance. The light resisted, yearning to dissipate. But I gritted my teeth and persisted. Again. And again.

Time blurred. I was lost in the impossible task. And at last... it yielded.

There, on the floor before me, lay the creation, faintly shimmering. A rope. Long, aglow with soft pearlescent luminescence, and astonishingly solid to the touch. I'd done it. I'd succeeded.

Now came the hardest part. Slip away undetected. Descend the sheer face. Reach the enigmatic South Archive. Discover, at long last, what awaited. Freedom? Or a deeper, deadlier snare?

Chapter 26: The Price of Hope

The hours until midnight dragged like chains through molasses, each second a hammer blow from a funeral dirge. I checked my light-woven rope again and again. The thought of rappelling down that sheer wall into an endless void sent waves of terror crashing over me. But the dread of exposure, the fear for Kaeden, burned fiercer still.

I'd memorized the guards' rotation. A brief window between shifts was my only shot. As Nocturne's deep subterranean night fell, I knew it was time.

I secured the Heart of Light carefully to my belt. Its glow might betray me, but I couldn't bear to leave it behind. It was part of me now—my last bastion of hope.

I fastened one end of the light-rope to the bedframe. It held firm. Slowly, silently, I eased the window open. Nocturne's frigid air rushed in like a specter. Far below, on an impossible depth, flickered the lights of the underworld city. The wall was smooth, implacable.

"You can do this, Elara," I whispered, steadying my trembling hands. "You *must*."

I draped the rope over the sill, squeezed my eyes shut, and stepped into the icy void. The first moments were sheer nightmare. I dangled on the ethereal cord like a spider on gossamer, the chill wind lashing my face. But survival's instinct surged. I gripped the light-rope—solid, to my relief—and began the agonizing, deliberate descent.

More than once, my foot slipped, leaving me swinging helplessly by my arms, panic clawing at my throat. But visions of Kaeden, his note, the fragile hope it kindled—they propelled me downward.

At last, when my strength ebbed to nothing, solid ground met my feet. An abandoned gallery. I untied the rope; it dissolved into wisps of light.

Now, to find the library. And the South Archive.

I crept through shadowed corridors, hugging the walls. Night in Nocturne teemed with ominous echoes. Twice, I dove into hiding from patrol shadows, heart pounding. Luck held.

After endless wandering, I spied the familiar arch—the library entrance. The door was locked, but a narrow unglazed window beckoned nearby. Summoning my dregs of energy, I hoisted myself through.

The library by night loomed even more sinister. Towering shelves cast writhing shadows on the walls. The air reeked of dust, aged vellum, and lurking peril. The South Archive... Kaeden had named it. I recalled the Overlord mentioning it housed the most ancient, perilous manuscripts.

I proceeded cautiously, footsteps muffled. The southern wing was dimmer, thicker with dust. The archive door stood ajar. I held my breath and nudged it open.

The chamber was a modest round vault, crammed with shelves of brittle scrolls. At its heart squatted a stone table strewn with maps and schematics. And it was utterly empty.

My heart plummeted. Had I misread? Had Kaeden failed to come? Or... was this the trap?

In the deathly hush, a rustle stirred behind a distant shelf. "Who's there?" I breathed. Silence.

Then, from the shadows, a dark figure emerged. Not Kaeden.

Tall, shrouded in a midnight cloak, he clutched a slender stiletto that gleamed with malevolent intent. "Caught at last, little fool of a bird," he hissed, voice iced with venomous spite. "Lord Kaeden bade me relay his warmest regards. And not to fret. He'll join you soon enough—in the Overlord's deepest dungeons."

A trap. Cruel. Unyielding.

The stranger advanced with deliberate slowness. I backed away until the shelves pressed against my spine. No escape.

And in that instant, it hit me. *Not alone.* The note's final words. Kaeden had warned me. He *knew* it was a snare. He'd tried to save me. But it was far too late.

Chapter 27: In the Embrace of Darkness, Hand in Hand

The trap. The realization hit like a glacial wave, stealing the breath from my lungs. The cloaked figure advanced slowly, savoring the moment, his stiletto glinting with sinister promise. There was nowhere to run.

"Who sent you?" I gasped out.

"What does it matter, foolish little bird?" He let out a serpentine chuckle. "Your flight ends here. The Overlord will be... disappointed. And your noble guardian, Lord Kaeden... oh, he'll pay dearly for his treason."

Kaeden. He'd tried to warn me. And now, he might already be captured. Because of me. The thought seared hotter than any fear. The icy paralysis shattered into a blaze of mad, unbridled fury. I recalled the Overlord's words: *Magic is will.* And I willed it—desperately willed survival. To fight. To save Kaeden. To let this bastard burn in my Spark's inferno.

I thrust my hands forward. The Heart of Light at my belt ignited in blinding brilliance. "Another witch with her tricks?" The man lunged, stiletto aimed for my heart.

But I was ready. A torrent of light—potent, focused, ferocious—erupted from my palms, amplified by the Heart's glow. It slammed into his chest. He unleashed a inhuman howl of pain and shock, hurled backward into the shelves. Tomes and scrolls rained down in a cascade.

But he wasn't felled. To my horror, he sprang up with unnatural agility, eyes blazing beneath his hood. "Filthy wretch! You'll pay for that!"

He charged again, swifter, more cunning. I dodged clumsily, scrambling to regroup my Spark. But he was too fast, too seasoned.

He seized my right arm in a vise that cracked like breaking bone. I cried out as strength fled me.

Then... a massive shelf toppled with a thunderous crash, billowing dust clouds. A shadowed form had shoved it with colossal force from the adjacent aisle.

Kaeden! He was here. Alive. "Don't you dare touch her, you scum!" he snarled. His familiar sword gleamed in his grip.

The attacker faltered, grip loosening in shock. I wrenched free and stumbled aside. "Kaeden!" The name escaped me like a prayer.

"Run, Elara! Now!" he shouted without glancing back. He plunged into lethal combat.

Their blades clashed in a piercing ring. They fought like enraged demons, turning the repository of knowledge into a battlefield. Kaeden was magnificent in his wrath—an unstoppable tempest. Yet his foe was lightning-quick, elusive. I couldn't leave him.

"Who sent you?!" Kaeden pinned the man against the wall, blade at his throat.

"You... you'll regret this, traitor," the wretch rasped. "Morven... he'll find you..."

Morven! So he orchestrated it all.

Abruptly, the cloaked figure twisted, a small poisoned dagger flashing in his off-hand. He struck for Kaeden's side. "Kaeden, watch out!" I screamed.

He recoiled just in time, but the venomous edge grazed his arm, drawing a crimson line. "You bastard!" Kaeden roared, fury unleashed. He knocked the dagger free with a savage strike, then clubbed the foe senseless with his sword's pommel. The man crumpled like a sack.

Kaeden panted, clutching his wounded arm. "Quickly, Elara—we've little time! The guards will swarm soon!"

He seized my uninjured hand, and we bolted for the exit. "But... where to now?" I gasped, breathless.

"As far from here as we can! I know a secret passage..."

We burst from the library. Kaeden led with assurance, though I saw him wince in pain. Two sentinels rounded the corner. "Halt! In the Overlord's name!"

Kaeden struck like lightning. Moments later, both lay in pooling blood. But distant shouts and footfalls echoed—the hunt closing in.

"This way!" He pressed a concealed panel, revealing a narrow, pitch-black tunnel. "In, Elara!"

We squeezed through just as the panel thudded shut. Safety. For the moment.

I slumped against the wall, gulping air. Kaeden wheezed beside me. "Thank you," I whispered. "You... you saved me again."

"I tried to warn you," his voice rasped, weary. "But Morven was craftier. He twisted my note to lure you. And me. He knew I wouldn't abandon you."

"Your arm... it's poisoned."

"Not now. Priority is escape. This passage leads to ancient catacombs. With luck, we'll slip away unseen."

"And if... luck fails?"

He gave a bitter smile. "Then, Elara, we die fighting. Together. But we won't yield alive. Never."

Gently, he took my hand. "Come, Child of the Spark. A long, shadowed road awaits." Hand in hand, we stepped into the gloom, toward a fresh, more terrifying unknown.

Chapter 28: From Darkness
to the Stars... and Back

The catacombs' darkness was absolute, a suffocating veil that pressed in from all sides. The air reeked of dust, mildew, and the faint, forgotten rot of death. Kaeden led the way with unerring certainty, his left hand gripping mine in a vise of reassurance. I could hear his labored breaths—each one ragged, the poisoned wound gnawing at him with relentless fire.

"How much longer like this?" I whispered.

"I don't know, Elara," his voice came muffled, strained. "This passage hasn't seen use in centuries. It could collapse at any moment. But it's our only shot."

I understood. Yet the dread of this choking void, the gnawing unknown, clawed at me. I tried to summon my Spark, but it flickered weakly, dimmed by exhaustion and terror. The Heart of Light at my belt lay dormant, as if sharing my fatigue.

Abruptly, Kaeden halted. "Stop. Water ahead." A soft lapping echoed in the black. "Part of the tunnel's flooded," he said. "Not deep, but we'll have to wade. Hold on tight."

The water was glacial, a searing shock that bit through my clothes. It rose to my waist, and every step on the slick bottom was a battle against the pull. I clung to Kaeden's hand, panic surging that the treacherous current might sweep me away.

When we reached dry stone, I shivered uncontrollably. Kaeden fared no better—his face ashen, the wounded arm slick with dark blood. "We need to look at that cut, Kaeden," I said. "It's bleeding badly. And the poison…"

"No time," he snapped, sharp with pain. "They're closing in. I can hear—"

Then I heard it too. Distant but gaining: a baying howl—or was it hounds?—and the thud of many boots. Nocturne's guards. "They know these passages?" I asked, horror rising.

"Some of them," Kaeden grimaced, wincing. "Morven knows every secret of this citadel. He's likely sealed all the exits. We're trapped."

We broke into a frantic run. The tunnels branched into an endless maze. When we paused to catch our breath, I pressed the issue. "Kaeden, your wound… Please, let me see."

He eyed me dubiously, but the agony etched on his face won out. He nodded curtly.

The gash was nightmarish: long and jagged, oozing viscous black blood. The edges festered, as if shadow itself devoured his flesh. "Dark magic," I murmured. "It's eating you alive."

I drew the Heart of Light. It kindled at my touch, responding to my plea. I held it to the wound. A gentle golden radiance enveloped the torn skin. Kaeden watched tensely, biting his lip bloody to stifle a groan.

When I pulled away, the injury had mended miraculously. The bleeding staunched, the swelling ebbed. "Thank you," he rasped. "I owe you again."

"We're in this together, Kaeden," I replied wearily. "If we don't escape as one, we don't escape at all."

He nodded firmly. "You're right. We move. They're too close." Something intangible had shifted between us. The shared peril, my aid—it forged a fragile bond, deeper than captor and captive, tentative as starlight in shadow.

The tunnel forked. One path plunged downward into musty gloom. The other, narrow and steep, ascended toward a faint gleam. "Down leads to ancient tombs," Kaeden said. "Deadly traps. Up... if memory serves, abandoned mines. Our best chance. If we want to see the stars."

We clambered upward. The shaft was so tight we had to wriggle like eels. At last, it widened, and I tasted it: crisp, frosty air. We emerged into a small cavern, walls glittering with embedded crystals. At its far end beckoned an exit—a jagged rent in the rock, framed by the true, twinkling stars.

Freedom. I drank in the heady night, tears tracing my cheeks.

But our elation shattered swiftly. We'd barely advanced when figures materialized from the gloom. Too many. Far too many. And at their fore, bathed in cold moonlight, stood Magister Illiriy. His porcine eyes gleamed with malicious delight. "What a delightful surprise, isn't it, dear Lord Kaeden? And you, sweet Elara," his voice dripped venom. "Did you truly believe you could flee the Overlord's all-seeing gaze? He was... most displeased by your betrayal. And commanded me to retrieve you. Alive. Or... alive. The choice is yours."

Behind him, Nocturne's warriors lazily raised crossbows. We were ensnared once more. And this time, no way out.

Chapter 29: In the Jaws
of the Unknown

Magister Illiriy's frozen words crashed over us like an avalanche, shattering our fragile hope. The trap had snapped shut. We stood on a narrow stone ledge, ringed by Nocturne's warriors, their crossbows trained unerringly on our chests.

Kaeden stepped forward, shielding me with his body. Even wounded and weary, he evoked a cornered wolf, poised to sell his life at a steep price. "Illiriy! What an honor," he drawled, venomous sarcasm dripping from every syllable. "The great Magister himself escorting us back? I'm afraid we'll have to decline."

Illiriy tittered, a shrill, grating sound. "Lord Kaeden, ever the wit. Even facing inevitable—and I assure you, exquisitely painful—correction. Our Overlord was most aggrieved by your betrayal. He tasked me with your retrieval. Alive. Or... alive."

"Betrayal?" Kaeden smirked. "I merely sought to safeguard the Overlord's valuable asset from your bungled experiments, Illiriy."

"How dare you, traitor!" Illiriy's face twisted in rage. In his palm ignited a pulsing orb of condensed shadow-energy. "You'll pay dearly for your insolence! And that wretched girl... oh, I'll have my own 'lessons' for her. I'll teach her true obedience. And suffering."

I felt Kaeden coil like a steel spring. We were cornered, utterly. "Elara," he murmured, "when I signal... run. To the crevice in the rock, left side. Don't look back."

"I won't leave you..." I began.

"Do as I say! That's an order!"

"No tearful farewells, dear Lord Kaeden?" Illiriy sneered with malicious glee. "Take them!"

The warriors advanced, tightening the noose. "Now, Elara! Run!" Kaeden cried, desperation raw.

In that instant, he did the impossible. He slammed his fist into the ground at his feet, barking a guttural, primal word that resonated like a beast's roar.

The earth quaked with a deafening rumble. The ledge beneath us crumbled, chunks plummeting into the abyss. "What in the hells?!" Illiriy recoiled in terror, his shadow-orb fizzling out. "Run, Elara! Go!" Kaeden shoved me toward the fissure.

I whirled. He teetered on the precipice, fending off the warriors who'd reached him. He was at his limit. And Illiriy was already conjuring a fresh, vaster globe of darkness. I couldn't abandon him.

I thrust my hands out, drawing on the Heart of Light at my belt. It blazed to life, heeding my call. I funneled every dreg of my Spark toward Illiriy. "Light! Let there be light!" The words burst from me unbidden.

A searing burst of golden radiance erupted from my palms. Not as potent as before, but enough to dazzle Illiriy and his men in a blinding flash. "Elara, no! I told you—run!" Kaeden's voice cracked with anguish.

But I was already dashing to him. I seized his good hand; our fingers intertwined. "We leave together, Kaeden! Or not at all!" He met my gaze, and in his eyes flickered something profoundly warm. "Stubborn, infuriating girl..." he whispered, a ghost of his old smirk softening the words.

We bolted for the crevice. Behind us rose Illiriy's furious bellows. We wriggled through the narrow, pitch-black shaft. Kaeden, despite his wound, moved with astonishing grace, urging me onward and upward.

At last, the passage broadened, and a breath of crisp air kissed my face. We emerged onto a concealed stone platform, cantilevered over the void. From here unfolded a breathtaking vista of Nocturne below. And directly ahead, in the cliff face, yawned another cavern. From its depths emanated a faint, alluring golden glow. "What... is this place?" I breathed.

Kaeden stared at the cave in bewilderment. "I don't know, Elara. I swear, I've never seen it before." Abruptly, a soft, ethereal melody drifted from within—like song or tinkling chimes. And the Heart of Light at my belt ignited, humming in resonance.

We exchanged a glance. Death's jaws had released us, but a new enigma loomed. "Shall we?" I asked, voice quivering with equal parts dread and intrigue.

Kaeden nodded slowly. "Seems, Elara, we have no choice but to press on."

Supporting one another, we stepped into the luminous cavern, toward an uncertainty that might prove salvation—or a deeper, deadlier snare.

Chapter 30: Sanctuary
of the Ancients and the Fury
of the Pursuers

The luminous cavern drew us into its warm, radiant depths, promising refuge and revelation. The ethereal crystal chime grew louder, like the song of unseen beings, its hypnotic cadence spreading a soothing warmth through my limbs. The Heart of Light at my belt pulsed in rhythm, its glow intensifying, illuminating our path.

The walls shimmered with bioluminescent minerals, alive with a mysterious pulse, casting a soft, pearlescent sheen. The air was pristine, scented with ozone and delicate floral notes. This place stood in stark contrast to Nocturne's fetid underbelly—a fairy-tale haven amid the abyss. "Do you... feel it, Kaeden?" I whispered.

He nodded slowly, awe plain in his eyes. "Yes. It's ancient magic—pure, profound. Unlike anything I've ever sensed."

We soon emerged into a vast circular chamber, bathed in gentle luminescence. I gasped in wonder. At its heart, like a pearl in an oyster, lay a perfectly round subterranean lake. Its waters were crystalline, aglow from within with a tender azure light. From the center rose a colossal multifaceted crystal, slowly revolving and refracting the rainbow's spectrum. It was the source of that enchanting chime that had lured us here.

"What is this wondrous place?" I breathed.

"I don't know," Kaeden replied in hushed tones. "It feels like an ancient sanctuary. A nexus of power."

We approached the lake's edge. The water was surprisingly warm to the touch. I gazed at my reflection and, for the first time in ages, saw not just fear in my eyes, but a spark of curiosity. Of hope. Kaeden knelt and cupped a handful of the glowing liquid. "Pure," he murmured. "Utterly pure... No trace of the Blight." He eyed his wounded arm dubiously, then rinsed it gently. With reverent awe, I watched the inflammation recede at once. Within moments, the gash had vanished without a scar.

I edged closer to the lake, toward the towering crystal. It emanated such pristine, potent energy that my breath caught. It mirrored my Spark, yet amplified a thousandfold. Compelled by an inner urge, I extended my hand. The crystal blazed with blinding intensity, the chime swelling to a deafening crescendo. My Spark surged in response, reaching out, merging with its force.

Visions cascaded over me. I witnessed the birth and demise of worlds, cities of light suspended in the heavens, exquisite races dwelling in harmony. I saw the first Light Guardians drawing strength from kindred crystals. And then... war. A cataclysmic clash with the Shadow that birthed the Gloom Blight. I beheld the final Guardians forging the Hearts of Forest, Mountain, and Water to safeguard the fading embers of light. And I understood... the ancient prophecy. Of the Child of the Spark, who would arise in an age of profound darkness to rekindle the dying radiance.

The vision burned so vividly that tears streamed down my face. When it faded, I knelt by the lake, trembling. "Elara! What happened?!" Kaeden was at my side, his voice thick with frantic concern.

"I... saw..." I stammered. "The past. The prophecy. I think... it's about me." I recounted it all. He listened, his expression darkening with each word.

"Child of the Spark... Last hope..." he murmured gravely. "The legends weren't lies. And the Overlord... he surely knows. That's why you're so vital to him."

"But why didn't he tell me?"

"The Overlord never reveals the full truth, Elara," Kaeden said with a bitter smile. "He doesn't just want to use you—he aims to shatter your will. And I fear his 'rebirth of Etheria' could doom this world worse than the Blight itself."

He traced the runes of the Light Guardians etched into the wall. "This place... one of their ancient sanctuaries. Perhaps the last. The Overlord didn't just steal their knowledge—he corrupted it. But this remained untouched. Hidden."

"But how did we find it?"

"The Heart of Light," he said, glancing at the glowing artifact on my belt. "It guided us here. It knew the way home." His gaze met mine. "Elara, what you've learned... it changes everything. We have more than hope now. We have purpose. Not just escape—but to fulfill that prophecy. And keep the Overlord from twisting you to evil."

His words rang with unshakeable resolve. He was no longer my jailer. He was becoming... my ally. But before I could respond, a guttural roar, shouts, and the clash of steel echoed from the tunnel. "They've found us!" Kaeden drew his sword. "Looks like our respite's over, Elara!"

From the shadows burst the Tainted. And trailing them, smirking with malice, came Magister Illiriy. "Ah, there you are, my slippery doves!" he hissed. "Hiding in a sanctuary? Playing at Light Guardians? It won't save you! The Overlord will delight in this little haven. And in learning his precious 'key' has found a new... patron." His eyes raked greedily over the radiant central crystal.

The Tainted charged with a savage bellow.

Chapter 31: Harmony of Light and Ashes of the Sanctuary

The savage snarls of dozens of Tainted crashed over us, mingling with Magister Illiriy's triumphant cackle. Shadowed forms surged from the tunnel, their eyes ablaze with feral madness. "Nowhere left to run, you wretched traitors!" Illiriy hissed, his voice a profane stain on the sanctuary's purity. "This haven will be your tomb!"

Kaeden raised his sword in a fluid arc, his face a chiseled mask of resolve. "Stay behind me, Elara! Cover yourself! And don't let them near the central crystal!"

We fell back toward the glowing lake. The crystal, sensing peril, throbbed brighter, its crystalline chime weaving into the clash of steel. The Heart of Light at my belt ignited so fiercely I feared it might shatter.

The first wave of Tainted descended. Kaeden met them in a whirlwind of flashing steel, his blade a blur of inhuman precision. But they were endless. One—a hulking brute with jagged fangs—broke through and lunged at me.

Terror didn't freeze me. I drew on every lesson etched into my soul. Thrusting my hands forward, I focused on my Spark, the Heart's radiance, the sanctuary's raw power. "Light! Let there be Light!" The cry tore from my chest.

A surge of pure, blinding energy struck the beast's maw. It shrieked, a piercing wail, hurled backward as its hide smoked and charred. "That's it, Elara!" Kaeden's shout cut through the melee.

But Illiriy snarled an incantation of shadow. From the roiling darkness around him formed elongated darts that whistled toward us like vipers. Kaeden parried two, but the third hurtled straight for my heart. I squeezed my eyes shut, bracing for impact.

It never came. The Heart of Light flared, weaving a shimmering golden barrier around me. The dart shattered against it, crumbling to dust. "What?! How?!" Illiriy reeled, shock twisting his features. Then greed ignited in his eyes. "It will be *mine*!"

He unleashed a torrent of black energy, vaster and more vicious. I raised my hands again; my Spark, fused with the Heart's essence, erected a radiant shield. The forces collided in a thunderous roar. The backlash hurled me toward the lake's edge.

Kaeden roared in fury, carving through the remaining Tainted to reach me. Wounded, he fought like a berserker, unyielding. Then I noticed the central crystal pulsing with frantic intensity, its chime swelling to a deafening peal. Its primordial energy flooded me, amplifying my Spark manifold.

"Use it, Elara!" Kaeden bellowed. "All the sanctuary's might!" I locked eyes on Illiriy, who was summoning another assault. I knew I had to end him. Closing my eyes, I surrendered to the fusion: the crystal's force, the Heart's warmth, my own Spark. Within me bloomed something transcendent—a perfect harmony of creation and destruction.

When I opened my eyes, my hands blazed so fiercely they seared the vision. I directed this cataclysmic stream at the Tainted encircling Kaeden. The light engulfed them—not merely incinerating, but enveloping in golden luminescence.

With a collective sigh, they dissolved into myriad glowing spores, which the earth eagerly absorbed. In their wake, emerald shoots pierced the stone, unfurling tender grass.

Even Illiriy froze, transfixed by the divine spectacle. "What... what have you done, witch?!" he croaked.

"I'm no witch," I replied calmly, a newfound strength threading my voice. "I heal."

Kaeden broke through to my side. "Elara, you... you're incredible!" he breathed, reverence in his tone. But Illiriy's stupor twisted into manic rage. "Foolish girl! You have no idea the power you toy with!" With a howl, he redirected his mightiest strike—not at me, but at the sanctuary's core: the colossal crystal. "No!" I screamed in despair.

The black beam lanced into it. A harrowing crack echoed, fissures spiderwebbing its facets. Its glow dimmed, the chime warping into a deathly keen. The chamber shuddered; stones rained from the ceiling. "What have you done, you madman?!" Kaeden lunged at the cackling Illiriy. "If I can't have it, no one will!" the magister shrieked hysterically, then vanished, melting into the shadows.

We stood alone amid the crumbling hall. The central crystal was dying. "We have to go, Elara!" Kaeden seized my hand. "It's all collapsing!"

But I couldn't tear myself away. Gazing at the fading crystal, anguish clenched my heart. "I... have to save it..." I whispered.

"Elara, no! It's too dangerous—you'll burn yourself out!"

I didn't hear him. I approached the lifeless monolith and pressed both hands to its icy surface. Closing my eyes, I poured forth my last embers of Spark, the Heart's every drop of warmth, all the healing essence within me. I gave everything, to the final breath, knowing it might claim my life.

A faint tremor responded—the crystal's timid flicker of light. Then... darkness swallowed me. Soft, warm, a lullaby of oblivion.

Chapter 32: Awakening of the Sanctuary and the Call of the Past

The first sensation pulling me from velvet oblivion was a piercing chill, soon chased by a longed-for warmth blooming from my palms. Hard stone pressed against my back, and a gentle hand brushed something sticky from my brow.

With effort, I pried my eyes open. Kaeden loomed above me, his face ghostly pale in the dim glow of the Heart of Light, which he cradled in one hand. Desperate worry swirled in his dark eyes. "Elara... you're awake at last," he breathed, relief flooding his voice like sunlight after storm. "Praise the forgotten gods."

I tried to sit, but my body rebelled, weak as wilted petals. My head throbbed. "What happened, Kaeden? The crystal..."

"You saved it, Elara. At the cost of your strength." He eased me upright against the wall and nodded toward the chamber's heart.

I gasped in awe. The colossal crystal had transformed. Jagged fissures had sealed, now veined with warm golden light. It pulsed with a steady silver-gold radiance, infusing the sanctuary with serenity and primal vitality. "It's... alive?" I whispered.

"More than alive," Kaeden said, draping his cloak beneath me for comfort. "When you collapsed, it blazed so fiercely I thought it'd bury us in rubble. Then... this renewal began."

The sanctuary had shifted too. The ceiling stood intact, unscarred. The lake's waters danced with a thousand golden flecks. Plants along the edges straightened, budding anew. The air hummed with floral sweetness and ozone. "You did this, Elara," Kaeden murmured, reverence in his tone as he gazed at me with wonder and admiration. "You didn't just mend it—you awakened its ancient essence. Restored the soul to this place."

I felt hollowed out, yet deep within stirred an unbreakable bond—to this haven, the living crystal, the Heart of Light. Kaeden gently placed the artifact in my hands. Its warm thrum now echoed my heartbeat. "Illiriy... he escaped?" I asked.

"Barely slithered away," Kaeden replied with a wry twist of his lips. "But he'll return. And report to the Overlord—about you, this place, what you're capable of."

"We have to leave. Before they come back."

"Agreed. But our entry's likely sealed. Though I suspect... this sanctuary's prepared another way." He traced a rune on the wall; a section slid silently aside, revealing a dark passage laced with crisp mountain breeze.

"Where does it lead?" I asked, struggling to my feet. Kaeden steadied me at once.

"No idea. But better than waiting." He searched my face. "Can you walk?"

I nodded, faint but resolute.

We ventured into the new tunnel—dry, temperate. The farther we went, the stronger the insistent pull. "Do you feel it too?" I asked.

"Yes," Kaeden affirmed. "Like something—or someone—ancient awaits us ahead."

The passage opened onto a stone ledge overhanging an endless chasm. Across the void, atop a sheer cliff, rose majestic ruins shrouded in morning mist. From there emanated the commanding summons. "What is this place?" I breathed.

"I've never seen it on any map. Hidden for millennia."

Abruptly, the Heart of Light in my grasp flared, and visions engulfed me. I beheld the city in its prime—a luminous Citadel of Light, soaring amid clouds. Its dwellers: tall, ethereal Light Guardians. And again, I glimpsed… myself, or one eerily akin, atop the central spire, radiating a brilliance akin to my Spark. Then—war. Flames, death, devastation. Shadowy legions assailing the bastion. And the last Guardian—an elder with silver hair and eyes brimming universal sorrow—concealing something vital deep beneath the crumbling foundations before darkness claimed him.

The vision snapped. "Elara? What did you see?" Kaeden's concern pulled me back.

I shared it all. "The legendary Citadel of Light… Stronghold of the ancient Guardians," he murmured. "If it's real, there might be something to aid us. An ancient weapon against the Overlord. Or knowledge to unleash your power fully." He eyed the abyss dubiously. "But how to cross?"

As if conjured by will, I spotted it: a slender, barely visible trail snaking down the sheer face, to a river below, then ascending to the beckoning ruins. "I think I know," I said, confidence threading my voice for the first time. Kaeden followed my gaze. "Incredible… You're right. Perilous, but our only path." He met my eyes, and in his flickered not just resolve, but true hope. "Ready for this, Child of the Spark?"

I glanced at the glowing Heart, then the distant ruins. Yes—I was ready. To unearth my past. To fight for our future. "Yes, Kaeden," I replied firmly. "I'm ready. Let's go."

Hand in hand, we stepped once more into the unknown.

Chapter 33: Legacy of the Guardians and the Ancient Warden

The descent into the bottomless chasm proved no less harrowing than our escape. The narrow trail crumbled beneath our feet with every step, demanding excruciating caution. Kaeden, despite his lingering wound, took the lead, testing each foothold. I followed close, forcing myself not to glance into the dizzying abyss where a mountain river roared far below. The Heart of Light at my belt emanated a soothing warmth, lending me strength.

Crossing the raging torrent was a trial in itself. No bridge spanned the foam-flecked fury—only slick boulders jutting from the water. Kaeden leaped across first with the grace of a mountain cat, then doubled back for me. His grip firm on my hand, he guided me over the churning rapids.

The ascent up the opposite, even steeper slope was torment. We clawed upward, grasping roots and rocky outcrops, until—utterly spent—we crested a grassy plateau strewn with the grand ruins of an ancient city.

An eerie silence reigned. Only the wind whispered mournfully through ivy-choked walls. Massive stone blocks, once pillars thrusting toward the heavens, lay in chaotic heaps. Yet even in this desolation lingered an aura of antiquity—potent, sacred. The air was crisp, untainted by the Blight's stench. And the Heart of Light at my belt shone brighter, its pulse quickening with joy.

"The Citadel of Light..." I murmured in reverence, eyes drawn to the spectral remnants of the high tower from my vision.

We ventured deeper into the ruins with care. The ancient city sprawled vast. We passed remnants of soaring temples, vast libraries, elegant dwellings. Faded frescoes adorned surviving walls: winged beings, epic clashes of Light warriors against Shadow spawn.

Abruptly, an irresistible summons gripped me—from that very tower. The Heart of Light blazed so fiercely Kaeden squinted. "It doesn't just know the way," he said with a grin devoid of its old bitterness. "It's in a hurry."

We raced to the tower. At its base, amid debris, ivy concealed a narrow entrance. Inside was dim and damp, reeking of dust and mildew. But as we crossed the threshold, the Heart ignited like a miniature sun, flooding a vast, empty circular chamber. At its center, on a marble pedestal, lay an open tome bound in blinding white, luminous hide.

With trembling awe, I approached. This was it—the Legacy of the Light Guardians. I touched the pages, warm and vital. Golden runes, myriad and ancient, kindled, bathing the hall in divine radiance.

Visions overwhelmed me, sharper than before. I witnessed the full saga of the Light Guardians—their wisdom, their creative magic, their desperate stand against the Shadow. I saw them forge the Hearts of Forest, Mountain, and Water. And I saw... the Overlord.

He was transformed. Younger. And to my horror, one of them—one of the mightiest, most gifted Guardians. Divinely radiant, with starlit eyes then still pure. But even then, a cold, imperious fire burned within. I beheld his downfall: consumed by pride and thirst for dominion, he delved into forbidden lore in secret. He sought to master not just Light, but primal Shadow, convinced it would forge true harmony. I saw his tragic betrayal. How, engulfed and twisted by darkness, he became the Dark Overlord.

The vision struck so viscerally I cried out, recoiling from the tome. "Elara! What did you see?!" Kaeden caught me.

"He... he was one of them... a Light Guardian," I whispered. "The Overlord... he betrayed the Light. He brought this Shadow upon our world..."

I poured it all out. Kaeden fell silent, his face ashen. "So the mad rumors... they were true," he said hoarsely. "I always sensed something... off about him. His hatred for the Blight— it's more than that. It's loathing for himself. For the monster he wrought." He approached the tome. "This book, Elara... it's not just history. It's their power. And perhaps the key to stopping him."

I returned to the pages. Now I discerned rituals of Light, methods to amplify the Spark, schematics for artifacts that dispersed Shadow. And mentions of other Hearts of Light, hidden across Etheria. If we found them all... if we united them...

The ground quaked. Stones tumbled from the ceiling. "What in the hells?!" Kaeden yelped, drawing his sword.

A low, guttural rumble emanated from an unnoticed shadowed archway. And from it slithered... something. Enormous, cloaked in dark scales, with multiple pairs of crimson eyes blazing. Woven not of flesh, but concentrated shadow. An ancient warden of this place? "Looks like we're not alone," Kaeden said grimly. "And this beast doesn't seem the welcoming s ort."

　　　　　　　　　　　　　　

The creature unleashed a deafening roar that shook the tower's foundations and charged.

Chapter 34: Dance
of Light and Shadow

The shadow beast's deafening roar reverberated through the tower, the citadel's sentinel filling the chamber with its scaled bulk. Crimson eyes oozed primal malice. Kaeden instantly positioned me behind him, his sword catching the faint light. "The ancient Guardians left a zealous guardian here," he growled. "Stay back, Elara! Be ready to unleash your power!"

The creature lunged, claws sparking against the stone floor. Kaeden countered with ferocious force, parrying a massive paw's swipe. The clash of steel on bone thundered, forcing me toward the pedestal with the radiant tome. My mind raced for a way to aid him. Fear gripped me, but I couldn't let him fight alone.

I shut my eyes, drawing on my Spark and the tome's freshly absorbed wisdom. I recalled the "Rays of Dawn"—focused streams of luminous energy to eradicate Shadow spawn. "Kaeden, behind you!" I cried as the beast's whip-like tail hurled him against the wall. He grunted, but sprang up, face etched with unyielding fury.

I extended my hands, envisioning my strength coalescing into a devastating beam. *Light! Aid us!* I pleaded silently.

A solar lance erupted from my palms, slamming into the creature's flank. An unearthly screech pierced the air; acrid black smoke billowed from the impact. The monster recoiled, its red eyes locking on me with hatred. "Well struck, Elara!" Kaeden shouted, pressing the distracted foe. "But it's still standing!"

Sensing the greater threat, the beast ignored Kaeden and charged me, fanged maw gaping wide. I fired another ray instinctively, but it twisted aside. It was mere steps away.

In desperation, my gaze flicked to the tome. Its pages fluttered of their own accord, revealing a sigil: interlaced radiant beams and circles. "*Shield of Light...*" I mouthed.

No time to hesitate. I raised my hands, mentally tracing the intricate pattern. The Heart of Light at my belt blazed with impossible intensity. As jagged fangs loomed, an invisible yet unyielding golden barrier materialized before me, mirroring the sigil's form. The beast's strike hit dead center. The shield quivered, cracks spiderwebbing its surface, but it held.

The monster bellowed in rage and confusion. "Elara, the eyes! Hit the eyes!" Kaeden yelled, flanking me. "They're its only weakness!"

I focused my Spark, channeling the Overlord's lessons on precision and control. Twin slender rays, sharp as blades, lanced from my fingertips, piercing two pairs of the largest crimson orbs. A heart-wrenching wail echoed. The creature staggered, thrashing blindly, smashing everything in its path.

"Now, Kaeden! Finish it!" I screamed, strength ebbing.

With a feral roar, he surged forward and drove his blade into the spot on its chest where a shadowed heart should beat.

The beast stilled, then unraveled—not into ash, but swirling eddies of gray, caustic mist that dissipated swiftly. Silence fell. Absolute, ringing.

We stood amid the wrecked chamber, breaths ragged. "We... we did it..." I exhaled, legs buckling. Kaeden steadied me gently. "You did, Elara," he said, awe lacing his voice. "That

Shield of Light... your rays... I've never witnessed anything like it."

I stared at my hands. A novel power coursed through them—not just my Spark, but the sacred essence of this hallowed place. Suddenly, the tome flared brighter; a page turned itself. Upon it materialized a new emblem: a double-edged sword entwined with luminous vines. Beneath lay indecipherable runes.

"What is that?" Kaeden asked, intrigued.

"I don't know," I admitted, bewildered. "But it seems our time here isn't over." Then we both heard it—a chilling, unmistakable sound. Distant, yet unmistakable: the war horn of Nocturne.

Chapter 35: The Path
of the Ancient Guardians

The piercing blare of Nocturne's war horn shattered the fragile hush. The merciless hunt had begun. We were prey once more. "They're here, Elara! Damn it!" Kaeden snarled, his gaze darting to the sole exit. "We have seconds!"

But I couldn't tear my eyes from the radiant tome, from the emblem of the sword entwined with glowing vines. Something in that sigil pulled at me irresistibly, whispering promises of answers. "This mark... Kaeden, look!" I whispered. "It's vital. My Spark resonates with it."

"Elara, snap out of it! We don't have time for riddles!" He strode to me sharply. "We need to get out before it's too late!"

"But to where?" I shot back in desperation. "They'll be waiting at the base. We'll walk right into another trap."

He fell silent, frustration twisting his features. He knew I was right. His eyes dropped to the open page. "The sword... and the vine..." he murmured thoughtfully. "It resembles the sigil of the Eldoria line—royal defenders of ancient Etheria. Legends say their blades were forged with Light magic, capable of slaying shadow creatures. But that lineage was eradicated... or so it was believed."

"Royal defenders... Ancient Guardians..." I stared at the luminous runes beneath the sword. The Heart of Light at my belt thrummed harder. And suddenly, I understood them—

not the words, but their essence. Images ignited in my mind. "Kaeden! Gods above!" I seized his hand. "These runes... I comprehend them! They speak of the 'Secret Path of the Ancient Guardians'! It leads from the heart of this citadel... to the Roots of the World!"

"The Roots of the World?!" He stared at me skeptically. "But that's mere myth! The nexus where all magic converged at Etheria's creation."

"The Guardians knew!" I pointed to the tome. "This sword... it's no mere symbol. It's a marker. The real blade must be here somewhere. And it will unlock the Path!"

The clamor of battle swelled outside. "Fine!" Kaeden decided. "If it exists, it's our only shot. Find that damned sword! Hurry!"

We scoured the chamber in frenzy. Where to seek a legendary blade amid these stone heaps? Instinctively, I attuned to the Heart of Light. *Please, guide me!* I pleaded wordlessly. It answered. A soft, precise beam lanced from it, illuminating an unremarkable wall. Closer inspection revealed a faint, weathered sigil—the sword and vine etched into the smooth surface.

"Kaeden, here! I found it!" I breathed. "The marker. But how to activate it?"

I touched the carving. Nothing. I channeled my Spark into it. Still nothing. "Perhaps..." Kaeden examined it closely. "See how the vine coils around the blade? Could be a mechanism." He pressed the hilt's depiction gingerly.

A soft click echoed, followed by a low grind. A massive stone slab in the wall slid aside, unveiling a dark vertical shaft plunging downward.

"Incredible..." Kaeden exhaled.

But triumph was fleeting. Nocturne's warriors burst into the chamber with bloodthirsty howls. And behind them loomed Magister Illiriy's twisted, venomous face. "They're here! Hold them! Don't let them escape!" he bellowed.

"Faster, Elara!" Kaeden shoved me toward the opening. "I'll hold them!"

"No! We go together!"

"Don't argue! That's an order! Go! I'll catch up—I swear!" He whirled to face the foe. I knew he was right, that I'd only hinder him. But abandoning him tore at me. I stepped into the shaft, then glanced back. Kaeden fought savagely, but the warriors swarmed. Illiriy was weaving a lethal spell.

"Kaeden! Watch out!" I cried. He turned for a split second, face slick with sweat and blood. "Run, Elara! Find the Roots of the World! It's our last chance..."

A warrior's blade struck him; he staggered.

In that instant, I knew what to do. I recalled the Shield of Light. I had to buy him time. Thrusting my hands out, I shaped the intricate sigil from radiance. A brilliant golden barrier flared between Kaeden and the enemy, blinding them momentarily. "Kaeden, now! Hurry!" I screamed, pouring my last reserves into it.

He leaped into the shaft, snatching my hand at the brink. Together, we plummeted into the gloom just as my shield shattered with a thunderous crack under Illiriy's incantation.

The slab slammed shut with a boom, sealing us from pursuit. Darkness enveloped us, broken only by our heaving breaths and pounding hearts. "You're... utterly mad, Elara," Kaeden gasped. "But... thank you. Again."

"We haven't escaped yet," I said, quelling my tremor. "Where does this path lead?"

"No idea," he admitted. "But it's better than back there." He struck flint to steel, kindling a small torch.

We stood in a narrow vertical tunnel descending into obscurity. Moss slicked the walls. "The Ancient Guardians weren't big on comfort," Kaeden muttered hoarsely.

"Not now. As long as it takes us far from Nocturne."

Supporting each other, we began the desperate plunge into shadowed unknown. Muffled through the stone's bulk, Nocturne's war horn still wailed—a grim reminder that peril shadowed our every step.

Chapter 36: In the Heart of the World

The darkness in the tunnel—which we hoped was the legendary Secret Path of the Guardians—pressed in like an endless void. The air carried the scent of pure earth, moss, and ancient dust. Kaeden lit his torch, its flame carving a narrow, roughly hewn passage from the gloom, spiraling deep into the earth.

"The Guardians weren't much for comfort," Kaeden muttered hoarsely.

"That's not what matters now," I replied firmly. "As long as it leads us far from Nocturne."

The descent was agony. The steps plunged steeply, slick with moisture. Several times, my foot slipped, and only Kaeden's iron grip saved me from tumbling into the abyss. His wound clearly tormented him—he winced with each twist—but he pressed on, stubborn as stone.

The tunnel twisted like a serpent, narrowing to claustrophobic squeezes before widening into echoing caverns. The Heart of Light at my belt gave off a faint warmth, its glow mingling with the torch's flicker to cast whimsical shadows on the walls.

In one cavern, our way forward was barred by a massive stone slab etched with an intricate weave of ancient symbols. "Looks like we're stuck," Kaeden said dubiously.

"Some kind of magical seal." But my Spark stirred joyfully at the sight. "Wait," I murmured. "I think... I know what to do."

I closed my eyes, envisioning my light tracing the interlocking lines, awakening their dormant magic. My fingers moved of their own accord, mirroring the pattern. Where I touched the stone, it kindled with golden radiance. As I completed the final stroke, the slab blazed and ground aside with a resonant groan. "Incredible, Elara..." Kaeden breathed, awe in his voice. "It was like you just... read the seal."

"I don't know how I did it," I confessed. "It felt like someone guided my hand."

We pressed on. The Secret Path brimmed with such riddles and snares. We traversed chasms via invisible bridges of light, navigated halls of treacherous illusions. Each time, my Spark—bolstered by the Heart and the tome's wisdom— unraveled the puzzle. Kaeden, with his strength and battle-honed instincts, shielded us from physical peril.

During rare pauses, we spoke. Of the Overlord, the Light Guardians, our fragile mission. "I always sensed a rot in him," Kaeden confessed one night, staring into the campfire's embers. "His obsession with 'perfect order,' his cruelty... it wasn't the Light's strength. But I was young, ambitious. He promised a flawless new world. Many believed. I... believed too." Bitterness laced his words like venom.

"But now you know the truth," I said softly.

"Yes." He met my gaze, heavy with regret. "And I swear, I won't let him wield you like he did us all."

These exchanges, this shared gauntlet of trials, drew us inexorably closer. I began to see beyond the ruthless Lord of Shadows—a man layered with tragedy, deceived as I had been, perhaps seeking his own redemption in the ruins.

The deeper we delved, the more profoundly I sensed our approach to something vital, ancient, immense. The tunnels' energy grew purer, brighter. At last, after what felt an eternity, we emerged into a vast cavern bathed in soft silver light. At its core, from a crystalline lake of flawless clarity, rose several colossal prismatic crystals, shimmering through the rainbow's hues. Their emanation—a pure, all-encompassing Light energy—stole my breath.

"The Roots of the World..." I whispered soundlessly, recognizing the mythic nexus from my visions.

But we were not alone.

At the base of the largest crystal stood a tall, slender figure draped in flowing white robes embroidered with gold, aglow with inner luminescence. A hood veiled her face, yet she radiated absolute serenity and boundless, primordial power.

She turned slowly toward us, hood falling back. Before me stood a woman, impossibly ancient—her face etched with wrinkles like the bark of an ancient oak. But her eyes gleamed with the same pure, wise, forgiving light as the crystals surrounding us.

"Welcome, my children. Child of Light and Spark. And you, my wayward but not lost warrior," her voice was a gentle murmur, yet it carried such resonant power and maternal warmth that it pierced the soul. "I have waited here so long, so desperately, for you."

Chapter 37: The Last Keeper and the Great Destiny

We froze on the cavern's threshold, bathed in silver light, words failing us. The woman at the central crystal's base turned slowly. Her hood slipped back, revealing a face mapped with deep wrinkles like an ancient scroll. Yet her eyes shone with the same pure, wise, all-forgiving radiance as the towering crystals around her.

"Welcome, long-awaited children. Child of the Spark. And you, my wayward but not lost warrior," her voice hummed softly, resonating in harmony with the crystals' subtle song. "I have waited so long here, at the very Source."

Kaeden tensed, his hand drifting to his sword's hilt. But I sensed no threat—only serenity, wisdom, and ancient power. The Heart of Light at my belt kindled a warm, welcoming glow. "Who are you?" I finally managed.

"My name is Liandra," she replied with a gentle smile. "I am the last Keeper of this sanctuary. Guardian of the Roots of the World."

"The last Keeper?" Kaeden stepped forward skeptically. "Legends say all Light Guardians perished in the Great War."

"Legends don't always tell the full truth," Liandra said, her gaze heavy with sorrow. "Some of us survived. We retreated beneath the earth to preserve what fragments of our magic remained. To await... her." Her luminous eyes turned to me with maternal tenderness.

"Me?" I whispered.

"Yes, Child of the Spark. You, Elara. The ancient prophecy foretold your coming. The one bearing the Life-Giving Spark. The one who would awaken the Heart of the Ancient Forest and restore hope to this world."

"The Overlord... he knows of this prophecy too," Kaeden said grimly. "And he'll do anything to twist her power to his ends."

"I know," Liandra nodded sadly. "He is the living shadow of our past—a child of my people who chose a dark path in the name of a perverted order. He will stop at nothing to claim your strength, Elara. And the power of this final bastion of Light." She gestured to the radiant cavern. "These Roots of the World are more than crystals. They are the primordial wellspring of all pure magic in Etheria. As long as they endure, our world can still be healed. But if the Overlord reaches them... he will either destroy or corrupt their essence, bending it to his will."

"But how did you know we'd come?" I asked.

"The Heart of Light you carry called to you. And I heard its summons. Just as I heard the desperate cry of your Spark when you awakened it in that ruined tower."

Stirred, I poured out everything: the glowing tome, the shattering visions, the Overlord's horrific truth. Liandra listened intently, her wise eyes reading my soul like an open book. "You have endured terrible trials, my child," she said softly. "And the hardest lie ahead. The Overlord will never leave you in peace."

"What can we do?" Kaeden asked, desperation edging his voice. "It's just us against his army of darkness."

"Sometimes, my despairing warrior, even two can alter history's course—if their hearts are pure," Liandra replied, regarding him with maternal understanding. "You wandered long in shadow, but I see light still flickers in your wounded soul. And this brave girl has kindled it anew." Kaeden averted his gaze, a flush darkening his cheeks.

"Elara," Liandra turned to me. "Your Spark is not merely a gift, but a profound responsibility. You must grasp its true nature. Its sacred bond with these Roots of the World. Its great destiny." She approached the largest crystal. "This is the Heart of this sanctuary. The chief Root of the World. Touch it, child. Fear not. Let it speak to you."

I hesitated, haunted by the ordeal of Morven's Starheart. "Trust me," she urged gently. "Here, nothing threatens you. This light is your ally."

Drawing a deep breath, I stepped forward. Kaeden lingered at the entrance, his eyes holding not just worry, but faith—in me. I touched the smooth, warm surface. A torrent of pure, distilled knowledge flooded me. I comprehended magic's weave, how Light and Shadow intertwined, how the Gloom Blight warped that balance. I glimpsed the Overlord anew— not just his past, but his hidden fears, his fragile vulnerabilities. And I saw the path. Arduous, perilous, but the only one. The other Hearts of Light, concealed across Etheria's corners. Each linked to one of these radiant Roots. If I found them... awakened them... united them...

When awareness returned, I knelt before the crystal. Fear and fatigue had vanished. I brimmed with otherworldly vigor, my Spark blazing brighter than ever. I knew my purpose. "I... saw it all... understood..."

"I know, child," Liandra smiled softly. "The Roots have shared their wisdom. And their final hope."

"The other Hearts of Light..." I murmured. "I must find them. Awaken them."

"That is your true path, Elara. Your destiny," the Keeper affirmed solemnly. "The only way to defeat the Overlord and heal Etheria. But it will be perilously dangerous. He and his minions will hunt you across the world."

"We'll manage," I said, surprising myself with the steel in my voice, meeting Kaeden's gaze. In his eyes burned unyielding resolve and unwavering belief.

"My dear Elara, we've truly taken on a mad new quest," he said, and for the first time in ages, a genuine, disarming smile curved his lips.

"I cannot join you," Liandra said. "My place is here. But I will give you this."

From her robes, she drew a small stone on a worn leather cord—softly milky white, emanating a comforting warmth. "The Shard of Dawn. An ancient artifact of the Guardians. It won't conceal your Spark, but it will help you master it. And guide you to the other Hearts of Light. Wear it always. Let it safeguard you."

With maternal care, she fastened the amulet around my neck. "Thank you for everything, Keeper Liandra," I whispered.

"Farewell," she said with a sorrowful smile. "This secret path will lead you far from Nocturne, to the Wildlands. Go in peace, and may the Light of the ancient Guardians illumine your way."

We gazed one last time at the shimmering crystals, at the wise face of the last Keeper. Then, with renewed hope in our hearts and a perilous new mission ahead, we stepped without looking back into the beckoning, daunting unknown.

Chapter 38: The Wildlands
and Ghosts of the Past

The secret passage spat us out into a canyon untouched by human feet for centuries. As we emerged into the open, the boundless, pristine Wildlands unfurled before us.

It was a rugged, primordial expanse, majestic in its raw severity. Endless hills cloaked in sun-bleached grass gave way to craggy ridges and groves of gnarled, ancient trees. The air was crisp and heady, laced with the sharp tang of steppe herbs. We were free. For the first time in ages. Yet that freedom tasted bittersweet—we were utterly alone in this unknown realm, with a mighty foe hot on our trail.

"Where to now, Elara?" Kaeden asked uncertainly, his hand resting instinctively on his sword's hilt.

I drew forth the Shard of Dawn. The milky-white stone around my neck felt warm. Clasping it, it hummed to life, a slender beam lancing from its core, pointing unerringly toward the misty northeast. "It knows the way," I said, excitement bubbling like a pioneer's thrill. "Liandra said it would lead us to the other Hearts of Light."

"Or into another trap," Kaeden remarked dourly. "Well, we haven't much choice. Northeast it is."

And so began our long odyssey. The first days were the harshest. We skulked in shadows, traveling only by night. Food came hard-won—Kaeden proved a skilled hunter, but game was scarce in these parts. I purified water with my Spark. We bedded down under the stars by smokeless fires.

Dangers lurked at every turn. One night, a pack of massive saber-toothed wolves descended on our camp. Kaeden fought desperately while I lashed out with bursts of light. We repelled them by miracle alone. Another time, we narrowly evaded a brigand's pitfall—spiked stakes at the bottom—thanks to Kaeden's uncanny reflexes.

Yet the journey held pockets of tranquility and wonder. I witnessed sunsets of impossible splendor, heard the trilling songs of mythical birds. With each day, I felt my Spark drawing fresh vitality from the wild essence around us, the Heart of Light at my belt pulsing brighter in response.

The Shard of Dawn became our steadfast compass, doggedly directing us northeast.

Kaeden and I, almost imperceptibly, forged a true partnership. He schooled me in survival's arts. I mended his wounds and cleansed our water. Our fireside talks deepened into confessions. I shared my visions and the prophecy's weight. Kaeden, in turn, unveiled fragments of his past. With aching empathy, I learned he was the last scion of an ancient but impoverished line, orphaned young and thrust into the Overlord's service as a boy just to endure. He offered no excuses, but I glimpsed beneath his armor of cruelty and cynicism a core of disillusionment, unhealed wounds, and a quiet yearning for a kinder life.

"I truly believed in him then, Elara," he said one evening, eyes fixed on the star-strewn sky. "Believed he alone could impose order on this dying world. I was so young. So foolish. And I paid dearly for that faith."

"But now you've seen the truth, Kaeden," I replied softly.

"Yes, Elara." He turned to me, a fragile hope flickering in his gaze. "Because of you. You've made me believe again that light endures in this world."

One afternoon, after a grueling march, the Shard vibrated fiercely, its beam flaring blindingly toward a distant range of forested mountains. "We're nearing our goal," I said, heart quickening with anticipation.

"Or fresh trouble," Kaeden grumbled, though excitement glinted in his eyes too.

By dusk, we reached the foothills. The forest here was dense and ancient, yet welcoming, exuding a serene, untamed power. The Shard guided us to a narrow trail delving into the woods, toward a shadowed cave. At the entrance loomed a colossal oak, its bark carved with symbols I recognized—the Light Guardians'.

"We're here," I whispered.

But before we could advance, a thunderous crack echoed from the thicket, followed by a chilling, all-too-familiar howl. The Tainted.

They materialized silently from behind the trees, encircling us. Their red eyes gleamed predatorily in the twilight. And at their forefront stood a tall figure in dark robes. Magister Illiriy. He had found us after all.

"What a long-awaited reunion, my elusive fugitives!" His shrill voice dripped venom. "Did you truly think you could vanish? I've tracked you from Nocturne itself. And now... your little jaunt ends."

He raised his hand, and the Tainted advanced with guttural snarls.

Chapter 39: Fury of the Pursuers and Wrath of the Guardian

The savage snarls of dozens of Tainted crashed over us, entwined with Magister Illiriy's malicious cackle. Shadowed forms surged from the underbrush, their eyes ablaze with feral madness. Illiriy led the charge, brandishing a black, smoking staff, his hands wreathed in swirling vortices of dark magic. "Nowhere to flee, you contemptible traitors!" he hissed. "This sanctuary will be your grave!"

Kaeden's sword flashed up in a seamless arc, his face a granite mask of defiance. "Behind me, Elara! Take cover! And don't let them near the cave entrance!"

We fell back to the mighty oak's base. The Heart of Light at my belt ignited so fiercely I feared it might erupt. The first wave of Tainted descended. Kaeden met them in a tempest of gleaming steel, his blade a whirlwind of superhuman speed. But the beasts were legion, clawing from every shadow.

I couldn't stand idle. Thrusting my hands forward, I summoned my Spark. The Heart of the Forest and the Shard of Dawn blazed in response, their pure energies merging with mine, amplifying it manifold. Potent lances of golden light speared the nearest Tainted, sending them reeling with shrieks, their hides blistering like flesh kissed by hot iron.

But Illiriy bellowed and hurled a colossal clot of black magic at me—a shadowy serpent vast as a river. "Not this time, witch!" I snarled, weaving a mighty Shield of Light before me. The serpent struck and hissed into dissolution against it.

"You've grown stronger, insolent girl!" Illiriy rasped, a superstitious dread creeping into his voice. "But it won't save you!"

He began incantating anew, deadlier still. Darkness coalesced around him like a storm. "Kaeden, stop him!" I cried, straining to hold the shield.

"I'm trying, Elara! But there are too many!" He spoke true. The Tainted hemmed him in; fresh gashes wept blood across his garb. Then the Shard of Dawn scorched against my skin. I realized: it didn't just empower—it could guide, transmute my light. I recalled the Heart of the Darkwood.

Forgive me... I whispered soundlessly to the tormented souls trapped within the Tainted. I redirected my power not to destroy, but to purify utterly. A wave of gentle, warm golden light enveloped the remaining beasts. Their furious howls softened to bewildered whimpers. From within, they glowed; the loathed darkness ebbed. One by one, they crumbled—not to black ash, but cascades of luminous motes. Where they vanished, fleeting visions bloomed: forest creatures, birds, even tear-streaked human faces, at last granted peace.

Kaeden and Illiriy froze, transfixed by the divine spectacle. "What... what infernal sorcery is this?!" Illiriy choked, his spell unraveling in a spiteful hiss. Seizing the moment, Kaeden lunged with a guttural roar. Their blades clashed in fury.

But Illiriy was no mere sorcerer—he was a seasoned swordsman too. He pressed the weary, bloodied Kaeden relentlessly. "I won't let you kill him!" I screamed, channeling a final, desperate ray at Illiriy. He conjured a roiling barrier of shadow that swallowed my light whole. "Your pathetic tricks hold no sway over me now!" he crowed triumphantly.

With a magical shove, he flung Kaeden aside; my ally crumpled silently to the earth. Illiriy advanced slowly, his smile one of victorious malice. "And now we're alone again, my stubborn Elara. This time, no one to save you."

I retreated until my back met the cave's rocky threshold. No escape. My Spark flickered, spent. Then... I felt it. A profound, ancient summons from the cavern's depths. The Shard of Dawn erupted in blinding radiance, searing my vision momentarily.

When sight returned, the ancient runes on the oak's trunk glowed with an eerie, verdant light. From the impenetrable gloom came a low, rumbling exhalation, like the breath of a slumbering colossus. Illiriy halted, his smirk crumbling. "What new trickery is this, witch?!" he croaked.

The ground trembled. Two enormous eyes materialized from the darkness, luminous with a deathly pale green glow. And a deep, primordial voice intoned, unearthly and resonant: "Who... dares... enter... here... and... disturb... the sacred... repose... of the Guardian... of this... ancient... Heart?"

Chapter 40: The Ancient Warden and the Song of the Mountain

The colossal eyes, aglow with a deathly pale green luminescence, fixed upon Illiriy's contorted face, twisted in terror. The low, rumbling voice carried unmistakable menace: "Who... dares... to come... here... and... disturb... my eternal... repose?"

The Magister recoiled. This smug servant of Nocturne finally grasped the antiquity and peril before him. "Guardian...? The Ancient Warden of this Heart...?" he rasped through gritted teeth. "So the legends spoke true..." His gaze flicked back to the entity, fear mingling with a predatory gleam. "What fortune! The Overlord will rejoice when I deliver not just this girl, but you, ancient beast! And the priceless Heart you so foolishly guard!"

Mad with greed, he raised his hand, summoning the dregs of his dark energy. But the Warden—this was indeed he—merely tilted his massive, stone-encrusted head in slow, disdainful contempt. "What a fool you are, child of shadow."

He made no gesture. Yet the earth beneath Illiriy erupted with a thunderous crack. Towering stone spikes burst forth at blinding speed, encircling the Magister in an unyielding cage. Illiriy shrieked, desperately clawing for freedom, but the spikes only constricted tighter. His shadowy magic proved impotent against the earth's primal might.

The Warden swiveled his enormous head toward us. His verdant eyes settled on me, then the battered Kaeden. "And you," his voice rolled like the whisper of ageless forests, "come not to destroy. In you, child—" he regarded me again—"I sense pure, unquenchable Light. The Life-Giving Spark itself. And..." His gaze fell to the Shard of Dawn and Heart of the Forest, "...you bear the marks of the First Guardians. So my sister Liandra, Keeper of the Roots of the World, lives. And it was she who guided you here."

"Yes... that's true," I whispered, fear ebbing into reverent awe. "She said another Heart of Light lies hidden here. That it must be awakened."

"This is the Heart of the Mountain, my child," the Warden affirmed solemnly. "It has slumbered for centuries. I am its faithful Warden. I have awaited the one—the chosen—who could rouse it. You are she, as foretold in the prophecies."

"But the Overlord... he knows too," Kaeden began hoarsely.

"I know of that wretched pretender who calls himself Overlord," the Warden interjected commandingly. "He is but a warped remnant of our past. A shadow that fancies itself light. His era draws to a close." With revulsion, he eyed the writhing Illiriy. The stone spikes tightened further. The Magister unleashed a prolonged wail before slumping limp in their vise. "He will harm no more," the Warden stated impassively. "But his master will sense this. And come swiftly. We have scant time."

He turned to me. "The Heart of the Mountain awaits. But to awaken it, your Spark and artifacts alone will not suffice. You will need all your courage to face its ancient echo. Its boundless pain. And its unbreakable hope."

"What must I do?" I asked, a desperate resolve blooming within.

"Venture into the depths of this cavern," he gestured to the shadowed maw. "There you will find the slumbering Heart. Touch it. Without fear. Let your Spark commune with it in the tongue of light. But beware. The Heart's energy is infinite. It may grant you unimaginable power—or consume you utterly, should a single shadow of doubt linger in your soul."

Then his eyes shifted to Kaeden. "And you, wayward warrior, have served the shadows too long. Yet light still embers in your scarred soul. Your charge is to shield this child. Not merely from foes, but from her own uncertainties." Kaeden nodded silently, a newfound steel in his bearing.

"Go now, my children," the Warden urged with paternal warmth. "Remember—Etheria's fate rests in your hands henceforth."

Kaeden and I exchanged a glance. Dread still chilled my veins, but it now intertwined with intoxicating purpose. We had a mission. A goal. Hope.

We stepped into the shadowed passage. The Heart of the Forest and Shard of Dawn flared brighter, illuminating our way. "And may the undying Light of the Ancients be with you..." the Warden's voice faded behind us.

The tunnel burrowed ever deeper, into the mountain's core. The air turned arid and feverish, thrumming with pent-up energy. A low rumble swelled into the mighty anthem of the earth itself. At last, we emerged into the final chamber. At its heart lay something extraordinary.

No gleaming crystal. But a vast, living, throbbing organ of molten stone, iridescent in shades of crimson and gold. Waves of searing, indomitable power emanated from it. And it sang. An ancient, thunderous ballad of the peaks.

This was it. The ancient, slumbering Heart of the Mountain. And I knew, in my bones, it had waited for me.

Chapter 41: Song
of the Mountain and Gift
of the Lava

We stood at the threshold of the innermost cavern, the most sacred of all. The low, resonant hum emanating from its core grew tangible, vibrating through our very bones. At the chamber's heart throbbed a vast, amorphous stone, radiating an unbearable primordial heat. Fear mingled with reverent awe and an all-consuming curiosity.

"Remember what the Warden said, Elara," Kaeden's voice pulled me from my trance. "Don't fear its ancient pain. But don't be swayed by its illusory hope. You must be strong."

I drew a deep breath and approached the pulsing stone. Tentatively, I touched its rough surface. It wasn't scorching—it was... alive. Warm and velvety, like the hide of a slumbering beast. In that instant, the world dissolved, replaced by blinding light.

A torrent of pure, visceral sensations engulfed me. I felt the wounded heart of Etheria pounding in agony, its centuries-old torment from the Gloom Blight's scars, from the betrayal of those sworn to protect it. Yet through the anguish, I sensed its indomitable, primal strength, slumbering deep within. And its final, desperate hope.

My Spark responded instinctively, reaching toward the mighty, suffering Heart of the Mountain, merging with its essence. For an eternal instant, I became something greater than myself. I was pure, all-healing light. I was life itself. I was hope.

I lost track of time. I drifted in an boundless sea of power, feeling my own wounds mend—not just the flesh, but the soul's hidden fractures. Fear receded, yielding to serene, unyielding resolve.

Then I saw the path. Not a map or vision, but unadulterated knowledge. Where to seek the next, final ancient Heart of the World. Far to the south, in the flooded ruins of a once-great city. And I knew a new, even graver trial awaited there. Perhaps, too, a fresh spark of hope.

When I resurfaced, I knelt before the Heart of the Mountain. It still throbbed, but its light had shifted—calmer, gentler, aware. The ancient heart had awakened... and recognized me.

Kaeden knelt beside me, his face etched with awe. "Elara..." he whispered, "you... you're glowing. Like the sun itself."

I glanced at my hands in wonder. They shimmered with a faint golden aura. I felt... transformed. Infinitely stronger. "It's awake, Kaeden," I said, my voice steady with newfound certainty. "And it showed me the way. To the last Heart of Light."

I described the sunken city. "Legendary Aqualon," he murmured thoughtfully. "A perilous place. Ancient tales warn of sea monsters and the ghosts of its drowned inhabitants guarding the ruins."

"But we must go there, Kaeden," I insisted firmly. "It's our only chance."

He studied me with a long, probing gaze. "You've changed profoundly, Elara. You're no longer that frightened girl from Craydol."

"I still fear," I admitted honestly. "But now it's not alone. I have hope. And a great purpose."

He nodded solemnly. "Then south we go. To cursed Aqualon."

Abruptly, the awakened Heart blazed with searing brilliance. From its crown detached a small, round, polished stone the size of a pigeon's egg—hued like molten gold fused with cooled lava. It drifted gently into my palm. "What is it?" Kaeden asked, curiosity alight.

"I don't know," I replied, bewildered, yet sensing the immense energy pulsing from it. "It's its gift."

I clasped the stone, and a fresh surge of warmth, power, and assurance flooded my veins.

"Our adventures grow ever more intriguing," Kaeden quipped with a wry grin, a boyish thrill in his eyes.

But before we could ponder the discovery further, that hated, bone-chilling sound echoed from the tunnel once more. Nocturne's war horn. Far closer. Far louder. Far more ominous.

"They've found us!" Kaeden snatched up his sword in a flash. "And trust me, they didn't come alone!"

I felt it too. Not just warriors approaching, but... something far darker. More potent. Lethal.

The Overlord. He had come for us himself.

Chapter 42: The Choice
of the Child of the Spark

The piercing wail of Nocturne's war horn shredded the silence. Its ominous call reverberated off the glowing crystals, heralding inevitable doom. Kaeden and I froze, staring into the shadowed tunnel from which our pursuers erupted.

"He's here after all—damn him!" Kaeden's voice taut as a drawn bowstring. "The Overlord himself. He sensed this surge of power."

Nocturne's warriors spilled from the gloom, blades bared. Behind them slunk Magister Illiriy, face warped in malice, and Morven, a cryptic smile playing on his pallid lips. Then, as if darkness itself had taken form, He stepped forth.

The Overlord of Nocturne. He entered the radiant cavern with effortless grace, and the light of the ancient Roots dimmed in his presence. His eyes swept the sanctuary languidly, lingering on me, on Kaeden, and finally on the throbbing stone from the Heart of the Mountain cradled in my palm. "What a spectacle, my dear Elara," his velvety voice filled the chamber. "You've surpassed even my expectations. I always knew your Spark held boundless potential."

"Leave her be!" Kaeden surged forward in fury, sword leveled defiantly at the Overlord. "She's not your plaything!"

"Ah, my loyal Lord Kaeden. Ever the hopeless noble," the Overlord sneered with disdain. "Did you truly believe you could hide her from me?" His gaze shifted to me, heavy and probing. "And you, my sweet child—do you still fancy this power belongs to you alone?"

"This power is for healing, not enslavement!" I cried, a newfound certainty steeling my voice—surprising even to me. The Shard of Dawn and Heart of the Forest at my belt ignited in response.

"Healing... destruction..." The Overlord drawled with feigned boredom. "Such childish notions. In this world, Elara, there is only will. And the strength to enforce it. My will now demands you—and that intriguing artifact—return with me to Nocturne at once."

"Never!" Kaeden roared, lunging at him. The Overlord didn't stir. He merely lifted a hand lazily, and an invisible force hurled Kaeden back. He slammed against the wall with a dull thud and slumped to the floor, consciousness slipping away.

"Kaeden!" I screamed in anguish.

"Fear not. He'll merely slumber a while," the Overlord advanced slowly. "We shall talk. Of your promising future."

I retreated, hands thrust forward, ready to unleash a torrent of light. "Stay back!"

"Do you truly believe your fragile light can halt me?" He chuckled with pitying amusement.

With a casual flick, writhing dark tendrils lashed from the shadows toward me. Desperately, I channeled my Spark, amplified by the three artifacts. Blinding rays of light struck the tendrils, forcing them to recoil with hisses. But they were endless. The Overlord's power knew no bounds.

"You fight well, my dear," his voice deceptively serene. "But you fail to grasp the truth. Your light is so easily devoured, twisted, turned to malice." His dark magic pressed in, infiltrating my mind, sowing seeds of venomous doubt. Horrific visions assailed me anew: Etheria swallowed by the Gloom Blight, Kaeden tormented in Nocturne's dungeons. "No... stop..." I whispered.

"Yes, child. This is the fate awaiting you both if you resist," his voice cooed like a tempter's whisper. "But join me... and we shall save this world. Together. Light and Shadow. We will forge an ideal, harmonious realm. My realm."

He extended his pale, elegant hand. "Join me, Elara. Become my Queen of Darkness. And together, we shall rule eternally." His promises were devilishly alluring. For a heartbeat, temptation tugged at me.

But then I gazed at the warm, living stone in my grasp—the gift of the Heart of the Mountain. I recalled the visions of the ancient Guardians, their selfless struggle. Liandra's sorrowful eyes. And Kaeden—his desperate willingness to risk all for my sake.

"No," I said, my voice ringing with astonishing firmness. "My light will never serve your darkness."

Surprise flickered across his exquisite features, swiftly hardening into icy rage. "What a pity, child. I offered you a chance. But you've chosen suffering and ruin."

He raised both hands, and the cavern's shadows coalesced into a colossal, roaring vortex of black, surging toward me. I knew this was the end. My strength couldn't prevail. Yet surrender was not in me.

I lifted the stone from the Heart of the Mountain high. I gathered the dregs of my Spark, every ounce of will, every shred of hope. I sought not to strike. I sought to shield. To preserve the fragile light within.

The stone in my hand blazed—brilliant, blinding, as if the sun itself had stormed the cavern. An all-pervading golden radiance clashed against the encroaching void. A deafening cataclysm erupted, as if two irreconcilable worlds collided in their final battle.

I felt myself hurled backward, tumbling into an endless void. Then... silence enveloped me. And darkness. But this was no hostile Nocturne shadow, no poisonous Blight. It was different. Soft, warm, soothing. As if, after endless torment and wandering, I had at last... come home.

Chapter 43: Between Worlds

The darkness into which I had sunk bore no resemblance to anything I'd known. It wasn't the icy void of Nocturne. This was different. Soft, warm, velvety. It enveloped me tenderly, as if I—a weary child—had slipped into a deep, restorative slumber. No pain, no fear. Only infinite, divine peace.

How long I lingered in that state—a heartbeat or an eternity—I couldn't say. But gradually, sensations emerged from the silence. A faint tingling on my skin, like the brush of sun-warmed sparks. A quiet, ethereal whisper, akin to rustling leaves. And... light. Gentle, diffused, pearlescent.

With immense effort, I opened my eyes. I lay upon something impossibly soft, like emerald moss, beneath the canopy of a colossal tree that glowed from within. Its branches wove from moonlight itself, arching upward into swirling, iridescent mists that shimmered through the rainbow's spectrum. The air was balmy, intoxicating with the fragrance of unfamiliar blooms.

Where was I? I sat up cautiously. My body felt light, weightless. My hands emitted a subtle golden luminescence. And my artifacts... The Heart of the Forest, the Shard of Dawn, and the stone from the Heart of the Mountain pulsed with a soft, rhythmic glow. They thrummed in perfect, divine harmony.

I was no longer in the shattered sanctuary. I was... elsewhere. In another world? I rose. Through the rainbow haze, ghostly silhouettes flickered: endless mountain ranges, radiant crystals, cities spun from light itself. "Kaeden?" I called. Silence. "Overlord?" More silence.

I was alone. Panic clawed at the edges, but I willed it down. I remembered Kaeden's words: *Control. It's your only shield.* I focused on my Spark. It was here—and transformed. Stronger, purer, more aware.

What had transpired in the sanctuary after my desperate burst of light? Had I transported myself here? Or had the stone from the Heart of the Mountain done it? I gazed at it hopefully. And felt a response. This place was its essence. The wellspring from which all Hearts drew their power.

Then the whisper returned, blooming deep within me. "Child of Light and Spark... You have come... We have waited so long for you..." The voice was ancient as Etheria itself, wise as the stars. No threat laced it—only boundless anticipation and sorrow. "Who are you?" I murmured.

"I am the eternal Memory of this world. Its inexhaustible Source. That which existed long before Shadow. And that which will endure after... if you fulfill your destiny..."

"To awaken the other Hearts of Light?"

"Yes... and no..." the voice whispered. "The Hearts are but keys. Fragments of primordial power. You must not merely find them. You must reunite them. Restore the sacred unity. Heal not just the land, but the very weave of this world..."

"But how? The Overlord... he's so powerful..."

"Darkness thrives only where light falters," the voice grew stern. "He whom you call Overlord is merely a twisted shard of what he might have been. He fears your light to his core. Fears you could awaken not only this world, but... his long-dead soul..."

Could even that monster harbor a flicker of light? "Seek, child..." The whisper faded. "Seek those who still remember the true history. Seek the sacred signs. Your path will be arduous... but you shall not walk alone... The Shard of Dawn will guide your direction... and the Stone of the Mountain will lend you strength..."

The voice fell silent. I stood alone, yet no longer adrift. Answers had come. And a new, more intricate yet profound charge: to bind the Hearts as one. To mend this world. And perhaps... to redeem the Overlord's soul.

But how to return? With faith, I regarded the stone in my hand. It ignited, surging fresh power through me. The luminous tree overhead shifted. Its branches intertwined into a towering arch. At its center, the rainbow mist parted, revealing a shadowed yet inviting passage. My way back.

I drew a steadying breath. I knew not what awaited beyond. But I knew I must go. "I'll return here someday," I whispered soundlessly, though I wondered if it were possible. Clutching the gift of the Heart of the Mountain tightly, I stepped resolutely into the dark, beckoning portal.

Chapter 44: Echo
in the Darkness and Ray of Hope

I awoke on the cold stone floor of that very cavern where the Heart of the Mountain had throbbed moments ago—or so it seemed. Now it was eerily altered. The mighty stone still radiated faint residual warmth, but its brilliant glow and resonant hum had vanished. Had it poured all its essence... into me?

An unnatural silence cloaked the chamber. "Kaeden?" I whispered soundlessly. No reply. Only the hollow echo of my desperate murmur.

I sat up with effort, my head spinning. Instinctively, I glanced at my hands. The familiar golden luminescence was gone. But my artifacts remained—the Heart of the Forest, the Shard of Dawn, and the stone from the Heart of the Mountain, still clutched in my fist. They pulsed faintly, in sync with my frightened heartbeat.

I was alone. In this empty, frigid cavern. What had happened after I unleashed my Spark against the Overlord? Where was Kaeden? What had become of him?

Reeling from weakness, I rose. Traces of the recent battle scarred the space: melted rocks, shattered swords, the acrid scent of char. How much time had passed? An hour? A day? I'd lost all measure. "Kaeden! Where are you?!" I called, but my voice only whimpered back from the walls.

I stumbled into the vast hall where the Ancient Warden had confronted us. The neutralized Illiriy was gone. The Warden himself, vanished. Only jagged stone spikes protruded from the floor like grim sentinels. Panic surged anew. Had they taken Kaeden?

I forced calm upon myself. I recalled the soft, wise voice: *You are not alone... The Shard of Dawn will show the way...*

Fumbling, I drew forth the Shard of Dawn. It was warm—feverish, even. I closed my eyes and, gathering the remnants of my Spark, reached out mentally for Kaeden.

At first—silence. Oppressive, suffocating. Then... a faint, spectral echo. Not here. Far away. Beyond this mountain. Outside. I opened my eyes. A slender golden beam from the Shard's core no longer pointed to our entry passage, but to another—faintly visible—the secret path Liandra had revealed. Had Kaeden, unable to find me, assumed me lost and fled that way? Was he waiting out there, free?

The wild notion ignited like a spark, bestowing hope. I hastened toward the escape route. The journey felt brief—desperate hope propelled me. I burst from the stifling tunnel... onto that rocky ledge overlooking the bottomless gorge. But Kaeden was nowhere.

In despair, I scanned the expanse. Nothing. Only the wind howled through the crags. Where could he have gone? I consulted the Shard again. Its beam now pointed stubbornly downward, along the treacherous trail we'd descended with such toil. Had he backtracked? Why?

Doubts gnawed at me. Yet I knew I must trust him. And the Shard. The descent was grueling. I was frail, teetering on exhaustion. But thoughts of Kaeden lent me strength.

When I staggered to the bank of the roaring mountain river, I saw him. He sat on a boulder by the water, head buried in his hands. His cloak hung in tatters, fresh scratches marred his face. "Kaeden! Oh, Kaeden!" I cried, hurling myself toward him.

He lifted his head slowly, and relief washed over his haggard features, squeezing my heart with ache. "Elara... it's you..." He lurched to his feet, eyes brimming with tenderness. "You're alive! I dared not hope..."

He didn't finish. In a few strides, he enveloped me in a fierce, desperate embrace. I froze for a heartbeat, then clung back, pressing my face to his shoulder.

"I thought I'd lost you forever," he murmured. "When that explosion hit... you just vanished. The Overlord was in a frenzy of rage! He commanded a search of every stone, but you were gone."

"I don't even know where I was," I confessed softly. "Some strange, luminous place. And there... an ancient, wise voice spoke to me. About the Hearts. About my destiny."

We parted slightly, but his hands remained firm on my shoulders. "You've changed, Elara," he said in wonder. "Your eyes... they shine differently. Deeper. Wiser."

I recounted everything from that enigmatic realm. My new, more intricate mission—not just to awaken, but to unite all the Hearts of Light.

"So Liandra was right," he said hoarsely. "And the prophecy... it's real." He raked a hand through his hair in frustration. "The Overlord sensed something too. After you vanished, his obsession to find you intensified. He believes you're the key to his supremacy. He's already unleashed his finest hunters across Etheria."

"We must hurry," I urged. "To the Sunken City. To Aqualon."

"Yes," Kaeden nodded resolutely. "But first, we escape these mountains. Find shelter. Illiriy and his warriors are still near."

He eyed the river with concern. "Looks like we'll rely on this water's mercy again to mask our trail."

He took my hand once more. "Well then, Child of Light and Spark—are you ready for more adventures?"

I met his weary yet achingly familiar gaze. For the first time in ages, I smiled genuinely. "With you, my wayward but steadfast warrior—to the edge of this dying world. Into the heart of darkness itself."

He grinned back, a mischievous, boyish spark in his eyes. "Then onward, my brave Elara. Great deeds await."

Together once more, with a fiercer hope burning in our hearts and a shared, sacred purpose, we stepped into the alluring yet daunting unknown. And the Shard of Dawn at my throat, as if in approval, flared brightly and pointed unerringly toward the distant, mythical south—to the flooded secrets of legendary Aqualon.

Chapter 45: In the Wildlands

The Wildlands greeted us with a harsh, primordial silence that was intoxicating in its vastness. We pressed southward, led by the Shard of Dawn's steady glow. Towering mountains faded behind us, yielding to endless rolling plains. The sky loomed immense and unyielding, a bottomless vault. For the first time in ages, I truly felt the expanse. An exhilarating freedom, though shadowed by the certainty of pursuit.

Kaeden proved an indispensable companion. His survival instincts, honed by years of service, saved us from starvation and peril time and again. He could read tracks like a book, knew which roots and herbs were safe to forage. From nothing, he conjured smokeless fires or sturdy shelters.

I strove to be a worthy partner. My Spark, empowered by the artifacts, purified water and mended our ceaseless scrapes and bruises. At times, I even ventured to wield it against swarming insects or to coax the plants around our camp into quicker growth.

The Shard of Dawn served as our faithful compass, resolutely pointing northeast—toward the flooded ruins of Aqualon, as my visions foretold. It would hum warnings of imminent threats: a wolf pack's approach or a Nocturne patrol's shadow.

More than once, we veered in frantic haste, holing up for days in ravines and thickets. Those taut moments of peril only drew us closer. We learned to read each other without words, to trust unspoken instincts.

Long nights by the fire under that star-drenched canopy became oases not just of rest, but of raw honesty. I began to unburden my fears to him. To my surprise, he listened with unwavering attention, never judging. In his sparse words of encouragement, I found more solace than in all the gleaming artifacts combined.

As we journeyed south, the steppe gave way to dense forests, then fetid, treacherous marshes. Game grew plentiful here, but so did the hazards. One day, I stumbled into a sucking quagmire, sinking fast. The Stone of the Mountain in my hand flared hot, and the mud around me solidified in an instant, forming a firm path that let me scramble free. "You've got your own pocket earth-shaper now," Kaeden quipped with a wry grin. "Handy little thing."

One evening, as despair over a dry camp gnawed at us, the Shard guided us to a forgotten islet amid the mire. There stood a small, weathered log hut—ramshackle, yet inhabited. "Who could live here?" I whispered.

"Anyone," Kaeden murmured back, hand tight on his sword hilt. "Hermits. Escaped convicts. Or worse."

We approached warily. The door hung ajar. From within came a low, monotonous croon—creaky and mournful, like a dirge.

Kaeden crept to the threshold and peered inside. Moments later, he straightened, genuine astonishment etching his face. "Elara, come see this. You won't believe it."

I leaned in. In the dim, cramped room, by a sputtering hearth, sat an impossibly ancient crone, withered as driftwood. Her face resembled the bark of some primeval oak. She rocked gently, bony fingers sifting dried herbs. But she wasn't what struck me. On the dirt floor sprawled a vast, yellowed map of Etheria. Glowing embers—crimson as fresh blood—marked key points. One smoldered here, in the marsh's heart. Another burned far south, by the sea, where Aqualon lay submerged. And a third, the most ominous, pulsed at the core of loathed Nocturne.

The old woman sensed our gaze and ceased her song. Slowly, she lifted her head. Her eyes—youthful and piercing, defying her frailty—flicked to Kaeden, then locked on me. In their depths, I glimpsed not just ageless wisdom, but a sly, cunning spark. "Well now, you've finally come, my long-awaited children," she said, her raspy voice laced with an otherworldly knowing and inexplicable warmth. "And here I was, sinful soul that I am, growing quite weary of the wait."

Chapter 46: Prophecies of Old Moira

The old woman's words—"I've grown weary of waiting for you here"—hung heavy in the stifling air of the ramshackle hut. Kaeden tensed, but I stayed his hand with a gentle touch. In this woman, for all her fearsome appearance, there lurked no menace. Only ancient, primal wisdom and a sorrow as vast as the cosmos.

"Who are you, lady?" I asked. "And how do you know of us?"

The crone let out a quavering chuckle. "Names are but fleeting winds. I am she who heeds the marshes' whispers and the stones' ancient songs. Folks call me Moira. And you—" her faded yet piercing eyes fixed on me—"you are the ones the winds of change have long sung to me. The bearers of this world's turning fate." She nodded toward the weathered map at her feet. "This path was not traced by my hand. But I can read its signs."

"This map..." Kaeden stepped forward. "Where did it come from? And what do these marks mean?"

"It found me long centuries past," Moira replied with a sly squint. "Many seek roads to the slumbering Hearts of the World. But only those who carry in their souls not just the Spark of Light, but boundless despair, ever truly find them. Or those who can point the way."

"You know of Aqualon? The Sunken City?" I asked, my heart seizing as I gestured to the mark by the sea.

"Oh yes, child," Moira sighed, her gaze clouding with memory. "A realm of unearthly beauty. And unbearable grief. The mighty Heart of Water sleeps there, in chill abysses. Its awakening will test you beyond endurance. For water remembers all—joy and pain alike."

"And this third point..." Kaeden indicated the mark at Nocturne's core. "What is it?"

A shadow crossed Moira's face. "That, my children, is the Heart of Shadow itself. The Overlord's font of power. Twisted, poisoned, yet inconceivably potent. Legends whisper it was once a Heart of Light. But betrayal's venom and thirst for dominion corrupted it."

"Can you help us?" I pleaded, hope warring with desperation. "Show us the way to Aqualon?"

"Help always bears a price," Moira said with a cunning smile. "These old bones ache from the damp. And my stores dwindle."

"What do you want?" Kaeden frowned.

"A touch of living warmth from your fire. A gleam of light from your Spark, my child, to chase the hungering shadows. And... share your tales with me. Old Moira delights in hearing of far-flung adventures and the winds of change."

It was an odd toll. Kaeden kindled a fire, and the hut warmed with comfort. I let my Spark bathe the room in soft golden radiance. Moira sighed contentedly.

And so we began our long recounting. Of captivity, the Overlord, the Darkwood, the Roots of the World, Liandra, our escape, and the new mission. Moira listened raptly, without interruption, offering only occasional nods or cryptic, prophetic queries.

When we finished, she fell silent for a spell. "Yes, my children... your road will be long and perilously fraught," she said at last, sorrow threading her voice. "The Overlord will spare no ruthlessness. And the ancient Hearts—they are not merely wells of power, but beacons that draw both light and darkness."

She rose and pressed into my hand a few brittle twigs bearing tiny, star-like silver blooms. "This is the Moon Tear," she murmured mysteriously. "Rare and enchanted herb. It will attune you to magic's flows and shield your mind from foul dreams and illusions. Brew it by nightfall. And remember, child—not all that is dark appears black, nor all that dazzles true light."

Then she turned to Kaeden. From her belt, she drew a small, near-black stone veined with a single, blinding white streak—like lightning frozen in time. "This is the Thunderstone, child of shadows. It holds no light's magic, but it absorbs and rebounds any dark force. And it..." Her voice softened, "...will ever remind you of who you are, even when your past's shadows seek to reclaim your soul." Kaeden accepted it with reverent awe.

"The path to Aqualon winds through the Foggy Marshes and the Siren Rocks," Moira continued, tracing the map. "Treacherous realms. The marshes teem with primordial beasts. At the rocks, heed not the Sirens' honeyed, deadly songs. Survive these trials, and you shall reach the sea. There, seek old Finn the fisherman—scarred across his face, eyes like a tempest's depths. Tell him Moira sent you. He may yet aid your cause."

"Now go," she urged. "Time slips from your grasp. And remember—Etheria's destiny hinges not solely on your magic's might, but on the strength of your hearts. And the choice you both shall make."

We thanked her fervently and departed. The night lay still, cold moonlight silvering the waters, stars blazing with uncommon fire. "Do you trust her?" I whispered.

Kaeden turned the Thunderstone in his palm. "I'm not certain. But she's given us a bearing. And a caution. That's no small gift."

I couldn't help but smile. For all the perils ahead, we had a clear purpose, a mapped course. And we were no longer adrift. The Shard of Dawn at my throat, as if affirming my thoughts, gleamed anew—its beam resolute toward the distant northeast, now steadier than ever.

Chapter 47: Song of the Sirens and the Salty Wind of Freedom

We departed Old Moira's hut at dawn. The path she had mapped plunged straight into the heart of the foreboding, untrodden Foggy Marshes. The name fit like a shroud. A thick, cloying mist limited our sight to mere paces ahead. It clung icy and chill, reeking of muck and something faintly sweet, nauseatingly so. Beneath our feet, black ooze squelched with repulsive hunger, ready to swallow any unwary step. Kaeden led, probing the way with a long staff. I followed in silence, treading precisely in his footprints.

The Moon Tear—the herb Moira had bestowed—proved a true lifesaver. I brewed it in my flask. The bitter draught scorched my throat, but my mind sharpened. The suffocating fog lost its malice; I discerned hidden quagmires and the jagged roots of marsh plants with newfound clarity.

Yet the marshes harbored perils beyond the terrain. More than once, we caught rustles in the reeds, glimpsed dark shapes gliding through the water. Once, a massive, ink-black serpent erupted from underfoot with a venomous hiss. Kaeden severed its head in a lightning strike before it could bite. Its black venom sizzled on the grass.

The Thunderstone, Moira's gift to Kaeden, found its purpose too. As we skirted a particularly fetid stretch where poisonous vapors spun dizziness, the stone hummed and warmed. Breath came easier; the rot's stench evaporated.

We pressed on all day, with scant pauses. Only as evening fell did the mist thin, yielding to a longed-for sound: the distant, thunderous roar of the sea. Then the shrill cries of gulls pierced the air.

The dreary fens gave way to a rocky shoreline, fringed by sheer cliffs where leaden-gray waves crashed in fury. These were the dreaded Siren Rocks, as Moira had warned. And then we heard them.

Their song—ethereal, divine, yet lethally seductive. High and pure, it pierced the soul, promising oblivion, peace, boundless bliss. It pulled inexorably. In horror, I felt my feet carry me toward the cliff's edge. The rocks and raging sea faded; I saw my beloved Craydol, sun-drenched and serene. Laughing children. Mother Greta's warm smile. And Kaeden, standing beside me, his face alight with joy, extending a tender hand...

"Elara! Snap out of it! Don't listen to them!" Kaeden's sharp, desperate shout yanked me from the honeyed trance. His features strained with effort; he battled the enchantment with every fiber. "Sirens..." I whispered, my heart pounding with terror and sharp longing for the unattainable.

"Their songs poison the mind," he gritted out. "We need to plug our ears—now." He glanced hopefully at the Thunderstone. It vibrated, and the enchanting melody warped, dimming for a breath, stripped of its fatal allure. "It's... countering them?" I asked.

"Trying to," Kaeden focused, channeling the stone's energy against the hypnotic pull. "But it's not enough. We have to cross this stretch as fast as we can."

I sipped more of the Moon Tear infusion. The bitterness sobered me, though the sirens' voices still echoed in my skull, tempting with visions of home, respite, forbidden love. Hand in hand—gripping so fiercely it hurt—we advanced along the precipice. More than once, I caught myself turning toward the sea, my steps faltering. But Kaeden was always there. His unyielding hold anchored me against the abyss of sweet delusions. At times, he barked something—harsh, abrupt—just to shatter the divine, deadly melody.

At last, the cliffs sloped downward, and the sirens' song faded into the surf's roar. We emerged onto a broad, desolate sandy beach. We had survived.

I collapsed onto the damp sand, gulping the fresh, briny air. Kaeden stood sentinel beside me, his silhouette stark against the sunset sea. "Well, we've reached the waves, my brave Child of the Spark," he said, voice roughened by strain. "Now to find this mythical Old Finn of yours. And pray he knows the way to sunken Aqualon."

I gazed at the endless ocean, its vastness both awe-inspiring and unnerving. Somewhere beneath those cold swells awaited the next Heart of Light. Abruptly, Kaeden stiffened. "Look, Elara!"

I followed his stare. Far on the horizon bobbed a tiny, solitary black sail, racing toward our shore with unnatural speed. Ally? Or yet another merciless foe?

Chapter 48: The "Sea Star" and Old Finn

The solitary black sail sharpened into focus. It belonged to a sleek, swift vessel. Its tarred hulls gleamed predatorily in the dying sun's rays. No flag flew.

"What do we do?" I asked Kaeden, my heart hammering painfully.

"We hide," he replied curtly. "Over there, behind those rocks. We'll see who they are from cover. If it's a Nocturne patrol, they'll scour the shore. If they're peaceful fishermen... we might get lucky."

We slipped into a crevice amid the boulders. The ship dropped anchor a mere fifty paces from the surf line. A dozen weathered, hard-bitten men spilled onto the deck, armed to the teeth with cutlasses and boarding axes. They lowered a boat and rowed toward the beach.

"They don't look much like Nocturne soldiers," Kaeden muttered. "Too ragtag."

"Could they be Old Finn's people?" I ventured, clinging to desperate hope.

"Don't count on it," he whispered.

The boat grounded in the sand. Four men disembarked. One—a towering giant with a thick gray beard and a black eyepatch—clearly commanded. "No one's here, Captain," one of his crew said in disappointment.

"Strange..." the one-eyed captain rumbled, his voice like grinding stones. "Old Witch Moira rarely errs. She said they'd be waiting right here."

Moira! It was them! I started to leap out, but Kaeden held me fast. "Maybe we beat them here, Cap'n?" another sailor suggested. "Or the local beasts got 'em."

"Perhaps. But we check anyway. If the Child of the Spark is here, we can't abandon her. That's the pact we made with the last Guardians."

Guardians! They weren't mere fishermen!

I glanced at Kaeden in astonishment. Awe flickered in his eyes. "I think it's time to show ourselves," I said firmly.

We emerged slowly from hiding. The sailors drew weapons in a flash. "Wait!" I cried, hands raised. "We're not enemies! Moira sent us! We're looking for Old Finn!"

The one-eyed captain lowered his cutlass deliberately. "Old Moira, eh?" He scrutinized me, then Kaeden. His gaze lingered on the Shard of Dawn and the glowing Heart of the Forest. "Well, that explains a lot. Which of you two is the legendary Child of the Spark?"

"That's me," I replied, summoning all my resolve.

The captain approached. He loomed even taller up close, more imposing. He smelled of salt, fish, and rum. "And who's this brooding shadow with you, lass?" He jerked his chin dismissively at Kaeden.

"He's my truest friend and protector," I shot back defiantly. "He helped me escape the heart of Nocturne itself."

"From Nocturne proper, you say?" The captain arched a brow in surprise. "That changes things." He grinned, revealing sturdy, yellowed teeth. "Name's Finnegan, but folks just call me Finn. And aye, I've got that famous scar across my face—hidden under the beard for now."

It was him. "Old Moira said only you could help us reach Aqualon," I said.

Old Finn fell silent, staring out to sea. "Aqualon… the Sunken City…" he murmured with evident longing. "Haven't heard that name in ages. It's a perilous voyage, girl. The sea brooks no strangers, and that city's riddled with secrets and ruthless guardians. Many've sought it. Few returned. And those who did… weren't quite human anymore."

"But we must try. Etheria's fate hangs on it."

He regarded me again, sorrow etching his features. "Etheria's fate, eh… If the Guardians and old Moira stake their faith in you, who am I to argue? I swore an oath once. Looks like it's time to honor it again."

He turned to his men. "Prepare the boat! We've got new passengers—important ones!"

The crew obeyed without question. "And you, dark fellow," Finn addressed Kaeden once more, "welcome aboard the *Sea Star*. But if I catch even a shadow of Nocturne in your eyes…" He patted his cutlass hilt meaningfully.

"I've long forsaken Nocturne and its mad Overlord," Kaeden replied evenly. "My loyalty belongs to her alone. And her quest."

Finn grunted. "We'll see. The sea sorts truth from lies in its own way."

We clambered into the boat. Soon, we climbed the ladder onto their proud vessel, the *Sea Star*. Sails billowed with wind, and the ship veered southward, bearing us toward fresh perils and fragile hopes.

I stood on deck, gripping the salt-crusted rigging. The Shard of Dawn at my throat thrummed ever stronger, its beam pointing unerringly ahead. Legendary, submerged Aqualon awaited.

Chapter 49: The "Sea Star" and the Salty Wind of Freedom

The *Sea Star*, our unexpected ark, proved sturdier and swifter than she appeared. Her great sail greedily caught the briny sea wind. The weathered deck creaked like an old friend underfoot. The very air thrummed with the invigorating scent of ocean, tarred ropes, and something intangible—the aroma of freedom, distant voyages, and impossible adventures.

Old Finn's crew numbered a dozen hardened, salt-lashed sailors. Their faces bore the etched lines of storms and scars—silent chronicles of countless battles. They spoke little, but every motion radiated the unshakeable poise of seasoned sea wolves.

The first few days at sea tested me mercilessly. Ruthless seasickness twisted my gut until I could scarcely stand. Kaeden, to my surprise, weathered the swells far better. He stayed by my side without fail, patiently offering water, fetching the hard rye biscuits Finn swore were the best remedy for mal de mer. His quiet, steadfast presence meant more to me than any balm or words could convey.

Old Finn was not just a masterful navigator but an inexhaustible spinner of tales. On long evenings, puffing his pipe, he'd regale us with seafaring yarns. And, inevitably, he'd circle back to our enigmatic Aqualon. "The legendary Sunken City... Jewel of the South..." he'd begin in that gravelly timbre.

"Once a dreamscape of water mages, artists, and poets. They danced in harmony with the deep. Towers of white coral rose straight from azure waves."

"What happened to it?" I finally asked one night, unable to hold back.

"No one knows for certain," Finn sighed heavily. "Some blame a divine curse. Others, a catastrophic arcane mishap. And then there are the whispers: Nocturne's doing. They say the Overlord coveted the Heart of Water, enshrined in Aqualon's grand temple. But the city's proud mages chose to drown it all—city and selves—rather than let the artifact fall to shadow."

The Heart of Water... Moira and the Guardians had been right. It awaited me. "Have you been there, Captain?" Kaeden asked unexpectedly.

"Aye, lad, I have. In my reckless youth," Finn chuckled ruefully. "A cursed, forsaken place. Ruins choked with venomous kelp. Treacherous currents. And its eternal sentinels—they take no kindly to intruders." "Yet you agreed to take us," I reminded him gently.

"That I did, child," he sighed again. "I gave my word to the last Guardians. And to that old crone Moira. Truth be told, I'm devilishly curious what makes you so special, my bold Child of the Spark."

Bit by bit, I acclimated to shipboard life. I even lent a hand—scrubbing decks, patching sails, learning the knots of the trade. The crew, wary at first, thawed toward us. Kaeden, with his raw strength and soldier's bearing, earned their respect swiftly. As for me... I suspect they simply grew accustomed to the odd glow that sometimes emanated from my artifacts.

One night, we plunged into a ferocious gale. Towering waves breached the rails; winds shredded the canvas. The crew battled the fury with grim determination. At the prow, I summoned every shred of will, every flicker of my Spark, every pulse from my artifacts. I couldn't halt the storm—that was beyond me. But I wove an invisible, resilient cocoon of golden light around the *Sea Star*, cushioning her from the sea's wrath.

When the tempest broke, I collapsed in exhaustion, but our ship endured. The sailors regarded me with a mix of reverent dread and admiration. Old Finn merely nodded in silence, and in his eye, I glimpsed paternal pride for the first time.

Kaeden had changed too, over those days. The crisp sea air and honest labor softened his edges. A long-forgotten mischief sparked more often in his dark eyes. Our conversations deepened, laced with vulnerability. I sensed trust blossoming between us—something profounder still.

Then, one serene dawn, the lookout bellowed: "Land ho! Dead ahead!"

A shadowy ribbon etched the horizon. The Shard of Dawn at my throat hummed fiercely, its glow intensifying, arrowing straight toward that mysterious shore. "It's them," Old Finn whispered in awe. "The fabled isles of Sunken Aqualon. Brace yourselves—we're nearly there."

But as we drew nearer, horror seized our hearts. A dense, unnaturally black fog coiled around the islands. From its depths rumbled a low, inhuman bellow. "What is that, Captain?" I asked, an icy shiver tracing my spine.

"Don't know, girl," Finn clenched his fists. "But it ain't like anything I've seen here before. Feels like someone's—or something's—been lying in wait for us. And I fear this won't be a welcoming reunion."

The *Sea Star* inched toward the ominous black shroud. I felt the Heart of the Forest and the Stone of the Mountain quiver in warning, heralding a peril darker than any we'd faced.

Chapter 50: The Heart of Water and Its Silent Guardian

The black, impenetrable fog roiled over the waters like a living, malevolent beast. The ominous, guttural roar rising from the ocean depths grew louder, setting the *Sea Star*'s deck humming with dread. Old Finn's battle-hardened sailors stood mute, their faces ashen. Even the seasoned captain appeared taut with unease. "Never seen anything like this," he muttered. "It's no mere fog. Something ancient. Vile as sin."

The Shard of Dawn at my throat dimmed, but the Stone of the Mountain grew fever-hot, vibrating insistently. "We have to press on," I said. "It's there—what we're seeking."

"I gave my word," Old Finn replied. "But this'll be deadly. Stay close."

He barked orders, and the *Sea Star* eased into the sinister haze. Darkness swallowed us whole—tangible, suffocating. The fog chilled to the bone, sticky with the stench of rotting fish and blood. Visibility plunged to nothing.

The low roar swelled to a deafening thunder. It mingled with other horrors: inhuman whispers slithering into our minds, heart-wrenching wails, piercing shrieks. "Don't listen!" Kaeden shouted desperately. "Illusions! The darkness is breaking our will!"

I felt the foul mist clawing at my thoughts, conjuring nightmares—the Overlord's mocking laughter, Kaeden's betrayal,

Etheria devoured by the Gloom Blight. I clenched my fists, anchoring myself to the light of my artifacts.

Abruptly, the ship lurched violently. A thunderous crack split the air, and one sailor vanished over the rail with a blood-curdling scream. From the fog erupted something unimaginable: a colossal, writhing tentacle, sheathed in slick black scales and studded with throbbing suckers. It coiled around the doomed man with crushing force and dragged him into the bellowing abyss.

"Kraken! Cursed Kraken!" Old Finn bellowed, drawing his massive cutlass. More tentacles surged from every side, smashing the deck like kindling. Chaos erupted—a frantic, hopeless melee. Sailors hacked at the monstrous limbs, their axes thudding dully against resilient flesh. Kaeden fought shoulder-to-shoulder with Finn, his sword a blur of steel, severing appendage after appendage.

I knew I had to act. Thrusting my hands forward, I summoned my Spark. The Heart of the Forest blazed, banishing the gloom for a fleeting instant. I channeled every ounce of power toward the thrashing tentacles. Blinding golden beams lanced out, and they recoiled with venomous hisses. "Hold it, Elara!" Kaeden yelled. "Burn the bastards!"

But the largest tentacle struck the hull with devastating might. The *Sea Star* listed perilously, shipping water. Wood groaned and splintered. "We're taking on water! Hull breach!" someone cried in panic.

"Forward! At any cost!" Old Finn roared. "If we reach the ruins, the beast might shy from the shallows!" The ship surged into the blinding murk on her last gasp. I kept firing shafts of light while Kaeden and the surviving crew fended off the onslaught.

Then... the fog thinned. The monstrous roar ebbed. We broke through. Before us loomed the grand, mournful ruins of sunken Aqualon.

Towering spires of white, coral-like stone rose from the dark waters, their summits crumbled by eons. Half-submerged edifices formed a surreal labyrinth. A dead, oppressive silence reigned. Our battered *Sea Star*, wheezing her final breaths, slipped into one of the broad canals. "We... made it..." Old Finn exhaled, his cutlass clattering from numb fingers. Two crewmen lay grievously wounded; three we'd lost forever.

I was utterly spent, but we were here. In Aqualon. Suddenly, the Shard of Dawn ignited at my throat, its beam lancing toward the tallest tower at the city's heart. The Stone of the Mountain at my belt thrummed so fiercely I felt it resonate through my bones. "There..." I whispered. "The Heart of Water... it's in that tower."

But as our eyes turned to the spire, we saw it. Atop its pinnacle, stark against the leaden sky, stood a solitary, towering dark figure. Even from afar, I sensed the aura emanating from it—chilling, ancient, potent magic. This was no Illiriy. Nor the Overlord.

It was someone... or something... entirely other. An ancient custodian of this realm? Or a newer, more terrifying master? And this enigmatic stranger had waited here—patiently, eternally—for us.

Chapter 51: City
of a Thousand Tears

The *Sea Star*, our wounded vessel, limped into one of the grand canals threading the core of the sunken, spectral city. She was a wreck: one mast splintered, oak sides gashed by the kraken's fury. The surviving crew labored feverishly to patch the breaches.

The toll was grievous. Three sailors lost to the black depths. Two more, including the valiant Jorjen, lay sorely wounded. I poured out the dregs of my Spark to ease their pain, mending what flesh I could.

Old Finn, for all his weariness and grief, held his resolve. "This is Aqualon, my children," he rumbled, gesturing to the mournful, half-drowned spires of white coral. "The City of a Thousand Tears. Legends say you can still hear the faint weeping of its fallen folk."

I strained to listen. Beyond the lap of waves and gulls' cries, a subtle, otherworldly murmur ghosted through—sighs of sorrow, ethereal and unending. The shadowy figure atop the central tower lingered, statue-still, its silhouette stirring an inexplicable dread.

"Afraid we can't bring the ship to the tower," Kaeden said, surveying the maze of narrow channels and debris. "Too shallow, too treacherous. We'll need a boat. Small group."

"You're right," Finn agreed. "We'll hold here, mend the *Sea Star* best we can. You two..." His gaze softened with paternal warmth upon us. "...this is your burden. Find what you've come for. And for mercy's sake, come back alive."

We lowered a sturdy skiff into the water. Jorjen, whom the captain vouched knew these treacherous currents like his own scars, insisted on joining us. We glided through the twisting waterways. Silence pressed like a shroud. The water ran dark, opaque; I shuddered, imagining what lurked in its chill embrace. The majestic ruins were a haunting blend of beauty and horror in their decay. Marble arches had crumbled into the depths. Ivory columns draped in slimy kelp. Faint frescoes clung to walls, remnants of serene city life—markets bustling, lovers entwined. Everywhere hung the weight of centuries-old tragedy.

The Shard of Dawn at my throat glowed steadily, charting our course to the central tower. Yet I sensed another force—a hostile pulse from the shadowed waves. This ancient magic brimmed with sorrow. Lamentation. And in its grief, perhaps deadlier still.

"Careful," Kaeden whispered as we slipped under a half-ruined bridge, fronds of predatory seaweed dangling like snares. "I feel something lurking."

Jorjen gasped in alarm, pointing to the water. Dark, amorphous shapes darted beneath our hull—swift, unnatural. A school of them. Too many.

"What are they?!" I breathed.

"No ordinary fish," Jorjen replied, his face drained of color. One shadow lunged at the gunwale; the boat rocked violently, nearly shipping water. "Hold on!" Kaeden barked, sword already drawn.

I thrust out my hands, and my Spark answered, weaving a shimmering barrier of light around the skiff. The shadows recoiled in fright but didn't flee, circling like a pack of starved sharks. "This city has guardians, alright," Kaeden said grimly. "And they're none too welcoming."

We pressed on toward the tower, repelling assaults. Icy waves of energy battered us—chill blasts meant to capsize the boat and infiltrate our minds, igniting primal terror. But my light held them at bay.

At last, we reached the base of the colossal central spire. The main entrance lay choked with rubble, but Jorjen spotted a narrow passage at water's edge, delving into submerged levels. The enigmatic figure atop the tower had vanished without a trace. "Now what?" Jorjen asked, voice quavering.

"Seems we have no choice," Kaeden replied, glancing at me with quiet concern. "You ready, Elara?"

I nodded silently. Fear still gnawed at my core, but it mingled with intoxicating curiosity and the unshakeable certainty radiating from the Shard. We disembarked onto a slick stone ledge. The dark aperture greeted us with sepulchral cold and the reek of stagnant brine. "I'll take point," Kaeden said, unsheathing his blade.

"And I'll follow," I affirmed. Jorjen trailed reluctantly behind.

We stepped into the lightless void. The Shard of Dawn flared brighter, its beam pointing relentlessly upward, into the uncharted heart of the ancient citadel. There, far above, slumbered the Heart of Water. And perhaps the very figure that had watched us so long.

Chapter 52: Guardian
of the Sunken Heart

The dark passage into Aqualon's tower engulfed us in sepulchral chill and the choking reek of brackish water and mildew. Kaeden kindled a torch, its flame carving a steep, crumbling spiral staircase from the gloom—a treacherous ascent into the unknown. "The Aquilonians weren't big on comfort," he rasped, testing the first step. "Stay close, Elara. Watch your footing." Jorjen, our young sailor, swallowed hard but gripped his cutlass tighter.

The climb was grueling. Steps had long since eroded, forcing us to scramble, fingers scraping slick walls for purchase. Water dripped relentlessly from above; wind wailed through fissures like lost souls.

With every height gained, the ancient magic of the place intensified. It flowed like liquid—ever-shifting, mutable as the sea itself. Potent, yet steeped in profound sorrow. The Shard of Dawn at my throat thrummed ever more insistently, urging us onward and up.

At one landing, peril struck. As Kaeden's boot met the platform, dozens of poisoned bronze darts hissed from concealed slits in the wall. "Back!" he bellowed, shoving us aside.

The lethal barrage embedded in the stone mere inches from where we'd stood.

"The ancient Water Guardians took no chances with intruders," Kaeden observed grimly.

"How do we get past?" Jorjen asked, desperation edging his voice.

I approached the wall, tracing faint symbols etched there—like frozen waves. "Wait," I said. "I think I know."

Closing my eyes, I shifted my focus—not to light, but to water. Calm, flowing, inexorable. I channeled that vision into the glyphs. They ignited in a soft azure glow, followed by a subtle click—the trap disarmed.

"Not bad, Elara," Kaeden said, surprise lighting his features. "Your gifts go beyond the light."

We pressed on. The tower unfolded as a labyrinth of hazards: shattered ritual chambers, libraries where decayed scrolls crumbled to dust at a touch.

In shadowed corridors, isolation shattered. Whispers echoed like lapping tides; fleeting phantoms danced at vision's edge.

Once, a translucent figure materialized—a young woman in flowing robes, her eyes hollow voids. A ghost. Her aura carried such raw grief it stole my breath. She regarded us, then dissolved into ether.

"The unresting spirits of Aqualon…" Jorjen whispered, pale as death. "They're still here…"

At last, the stairs deposited us in a vast circular chamber crowning the spire. The roof had caved long ago, framing a brooding, leaden sky.

And there, at the center, upon a pedestal of translucent, ice-blue stone, rested it—the ancient, slumbering Heart of Water. A flawless sphere of purest, churning liquid, alive and effervescent. It rotated languidly, shimmering through blues and greens, emanating a pearlescent radiance and the primal force of untamed oceans. It sang—a crystalline chime, melodic and entrancing.

Beside it, back to us, stood the enigmatic figure. Tall and lithe, cloaked in a deep indigo robe embroidered with silver waves. She turned slowly. A woman. Of unearthly, haunting beauty—yet her allure chilled like abyssal depths. Her skin gleamed like pearl; her vast eyes mirrored the clearest sea swells. In their depths swirled not just timeless wisdom, but an all-consuming sorrow that pierced the soul.

"You've come at last, long-awaited guests," her voice murmured, soft as surf on sand. "I've sensed your arduous approach for so long. The arrival of the true Child of Light and Spark. And..." Her gaze lingered on Kaeden with quiet wonder, "...the valiant warrior, lost yet bearing an unquenched light in his scarred soul."

"Who are you?" I asked, drawn nearer. The Heart of Water tugged at me with inexorable pull.

"I am Amareya, Child of Light," she replied, a melancholy smile curving her lips. "Last of the priestesses of this once-great Aqualon. And final Guardian of this sacred Heart. Brave Elara... I have awaited you here for a very, very long time."

Chapter 53: The Last Priestess of Aqualon

"I have awaited you, Elara, for a very, very long time," Amareya repeated softly, her melodic voice filling the chamber like the gentle rush of incoming tides. The radiant sphere of the Heart of Water pulsed in rhythm with her words.

Kaeden remained taut, his hand never straying from his sword's hilt. But I sensed no threat. From this woman emanated serenity, wisdom, and an ancient power. The Heart of Light at my belt kindled a warm, welcoming glow. "You... knew I would come?" I asked.

"Ancient prophecies seldom err, Child of the Spark," Amareya replied with a sorrowful smile. "They foretold one who bears the Life-Giving Spark. One who would gather the lost Hearts of the World. I am but one of many who have awaited your saving light."

"One of many?" I echoed in surprise. "So there are other Guardians in Etheria?"

"Alas, child, few remember the old oaths," Amareya nodded. "With each century, our numbers dwindle. The devouring Darkness and despair are potent poisons. I am the last priestess of this Temple of Water. The final Guardian of this Heart. I remained when my beloved Aqualon fell, to safeguard its power until your arrival."

"What happened to this city?" Kaeden interjected sharply.

A shadow crossed Amareya's face. "Aqualon was Etheria's jewel. A haven of harmony, art, and water magic. We lived in balance with the ocean, drawing strength and insight from its depths. But then... the Shadow came." She fell silent for a long moment. "Not the Overlord you know, Elara. In those days, he was different. Young, brilliant, a mighty Guardian of Light. But his soul was already poisoned by lust for power and forbidden lore. He came to Aqualon, demanding fealty. Demanding we surrender our sacred Heart of Water for his dark machinations."

"And you refused," I surmised.

"Yes. We had no choice. Aqualon's brave mages clashed with him in desperate battle. We prevailed... but he proved cunning. In the final hour, he unleashed a forbidden incantation to seize the Heart. Something went awry. The spell summoned an unimaginable cataclysm. The ocean, like a wrathful god, crashed upon our gleaming city, swallowing it in an instant." Amareya drew a heavy breath. "I was among the few who survived by miracle's grace. I took shelter in this tower and have guarded its essence ever since, awaiting she who could awaken it."

"Awaken it?" My gaze trembled toward the watery orb. "Is it not alive?"

"It lives, child. But deeply wounded. It slumbers in heavy repose," Amareya murmured, her fingers brushing the luminous surface with tenderness. "Its power waned under the Shadow's assault. It yearns desperately for your Spark. For the purity of your light. Only you can restore its former might."

"What must I do?" I asked, resolve surging within me like a gathering wave.

"You must do more than touch it. You must enter it."

"Enter... it?" Kaeden and I exchanged incredulous glances.

"Yes. Fear not—the Heart of Water will receive you. Immerse yourself in its essence and heal the wounds inflicted by darkness with your light. But it will be perilous. Water remembers all: Aqualon's radiant harmony, and the agony of its doom. You must face that horror unflinchingly. And not break."

I met Kaeden's eyes, finding unyielding support there. "I'll be right here, Elara," he said firmly. "No one will touch you."

"And you, my wayward warrior," Amareya regarded him with gentle compassion, "your soul still wrestles with the light. But this Heart may aid you too, if you permit it. Its purity can wash away even the deepest scars."

"The time has come, Elara," Amareya intoned solemnly. "While Illiriy and his minions lick their wounds, we have this chance. Approach. And trust in this Heart."

I drew a deep breath and took the fateful step toward the glowing sphere.

The Heart of Water felt warm, alive. As my palms pressed against it, it erupted in blinding brilliance. An unseen force drew me in slowly, like the tide's inexorable pull, into its boundless depths. The world dissolved, replaced by a luminous ocean of light. I heard the whispers of waves, the songs of whales, the laughter of dolphins. I beheld legendary Aqualon in its splendor—ivory towers, pearl bridges, enchanted underwater gardens.

But the vision darkened to nightmare. Devouring shadow engulfed it all: the Overlord's silhouette, the frenzy of unleashed elements. Pain, despair, death. Horrific images sought to drown me in grief. Yet I held fast, clinging to memories of the Roots of the World's light, the Stone of the Mountain's warmth, the Shard of Dawn's gleam. I summoned my Spark.

And, unbidden, I began to sing. Not with voice, but soul. An ancient hymn of hope. Of all-healing light. Of eternal life. My song wove into the Heart of Water's mighty chorus.

When awareness returned, I knelt before the radiant crystal. But everything had transformed. The ancient Heart blazed with unprecedented fervor, its vital light banishing lingering shadows. The surrounding pool ran crystal-clear, alive with myriad twinkling stars in its depths. Amareya gazed at me, tears tracing her cheeks. "You have done it, child," she whispered. "You did not merely awaken it. You healed it."

I looked to my hands, aglow with warm golden light. A surge of otherworldly power coursed through me. My Spark had deepened, strengthened, grown wiser. The Stone of the Mountain at my belt flared crimson-gold, its essence merging with the Heart of Water and my Spark. No longer disparate forces—they had become a unified, inconceivably potent whole.

Then the ancient, ethereal voice echoed in my mind once more. *Two sacred Hearts awakened... The Great Path traversed... But the Shadow endures... and draws near... You must hasten... seek the final, mightiest Heart... The legendary Heart of the Heavens themselves... Only then, uniting all three... shall you...*

The voice cut off. The tower shuddered from a cataclysmic impact. Stones rained from the ceiling. From outside roared a new, deafening, inhuman bellow.

"What is that?!" Kaeden cried in alarm.

Amareya paled to the color of bone. "He... he has come... The Great Guardian of these Depths... He senses the Heart's awakening... And he will never yield it without a fight to the death..."

Chapter 54: Wrath of the Depths and the Overlord's Fury

The ancient, ethereal voice had scarcely faded when the tower quaked from a devastating blow. Debris rained from the ceiling. From the sea beyond came a furious, inhuman roar that set the canal waters boiling.

"He... has come," Amareya whispered, her face drained to ghostly pallor. "The Great Guardian of these Depths... He senses the Heart's awakening... And he will never yield it without a battle to the death..."

Before her words trailed off, the tower wall exploded inward with a deafening crack. Seawater surged through the breach, and behind it loomed the beast. A primordial horror from the darkest seafaring nightmares. Its colossal, sinuous body, sheathed in iridescent black scales, evoked both serpent and kraken. A shapeless head bristled with multiple pairs of bottomless, pitch-black eyes, ablaze with cold, otherworldly fire. Dozens—perhaps hundreds—of lithe tentacles tipped with chitinous claws writhed about it, shattering aeons-old stone with effortless malice. This was the Guardian of the Depths.

It unleashed another earth-shattering bellow, and one tentacle lashed toward the radiant Heart of Water. "Not on my watch!" Kaeden roared, lunging forward with sword raised. Jorjen, ashen with terror, stood resolute at his side.

Amareya flung up her hands. Water from the pool at the crystal's base erupted, forming a shimmering aqueous barrier before the artifact. The tentacle smashed into it with cataclysmic force. The shield trembled but held. "Elara! Aid me!" Amareya's voice cracked with strain. "This Heart is bound to you now! We must protect it!"

Terror rooted me in place, but the sight of my friends' desperate stand shattered the paralysis. I knew what I had to do. Stepping beside Amareya, I closed my eyes and focused on my Spark, on the power that had surged within me. I felt it merge with the Heart of Water's essence, with its ancient song. *Light and Water—together, now and forever,* I exhaled wordlessly.

A searing beam, woven of golden light and churning waves, struck the monster's head. The Guardian bellowed in agony and rage, recoiling instinctively as its tentacles flailed blindly, pulverizing the tower walls. "Hold fast, child!" Amareya cried, channeling fresh torrents against the beast.

Kaeden and Jorjen charged with frenzied valor, their blades raining blows on tentacles breaching our defenses. The fray raged. The Guardian was inconceivably mighty. Its scales defied penetration; its limbs struck with lightning speed. More than once, they nearly ensnared me or Amareya, saved only by Kaeden's desperate parries. My strength ebbed, but I gazed upon Amareya's anguished face, Kaeden's bloodied yet unyielding determination, Jorjen's pallid courage. I could not falter.

"Its eyes, Elara! Look at its eyes!" Kaeden shouted. "They're different! Not like the Tainted!"

I peered into the vast black orbs. No mindless fury burned there. Only... unbearable, cosmic pain. And a child's vulnerable fear. "It's... not evil," I whispered. "It's suffering. Afraid..."

"Child, snap to!" Amareya cried. "It's trying to kill us!"

"No..." I shook my head. "It's defending this place. Wounded. Just like the Heart."

I shut my eyes again. Instead of assault, I directed a wave of genuine compassion toward the Guardian. Pure, forgiving light. My Spark, fused with the Heart of Water's power, brushed its tormented mind. Through its gaze, I witnessed Aqualon's fall—the elemental fury, the encroaching darkness devouring all life. This ancient sentinel was woven into the ocean, the city itself. For centuries, it had endured anguish alongside them.

The Guardian stilled. Its wrathful roar softened to a piteous moan. Tentacles drooped limply into the waters. It regarded me slowly, fury extinguished from its eyes—replaced by endless, heartrending sorrow. Then, with deliberate grace, it bowed its massive head in deference. And as slowly, it submerged into the roiling depths, vanishing into shadow. Silence fell. Profound, surreal.

We stood frozen, words failing us. "You... you did it, my extraordinary Elara," Amareya whispered, tears glistening on her cheeks. "You didn't just defeat it. You understood. Heard. Healed."

I swayed, strength deserting me. Kaeden caught me swiftly. "Elara, you alright?" His voice brimmed with desperate concern.

"I'm... so tired, Kaeden," I murmured, eyelids drooping.

The Heart of Water shone with serene, soothing radiance, its crystalline song now divinely exquisite. The air in the tower seemed purer, cleansed. But our respite was illusory.

Abruptly, the Shard of Dawn at my throat blazed crimson as blood. The Stone of the Mountain turned icy cold. "What now?!" Kaeden tensed.

Then we all heard it. Distant yet unmistakable, a soul-chilling blast. The war horn of Nocturne. Not one, but many. An

armada. The almighty Overlord hadn't merely tracked us—
he had come himself. For the sacred Heart of Water. And he
brought his invincible legions.

Chapter 55: The United Hearts

The chorus of Nocturne's war horns shattered the silence, heralding doom. From the misty horizon emerged black, predatory silhouettes—one after another. An entire armada, dispatched by the Overlord himself.

"He's here after all," Amareya, the last Priestess of Aqualon, stood at the platform's edge. Resolve burned cold and unyielding in her eyes. "He comes for the Heart of Water. And for you, my precious Child of the Spark."

Kaeden growled low, fingers tightening on his sword hilt. "There are too many. We can't hold the tower." Jorjen, our young sailor, though pale with fear, clutched his cutlass fiercely. "We'll fight, m'lord. To our last breath."

I gazed at the radiant sphere of the awakened Heart of Water. It pulsed serenely, and I felt its boundless power, its mystical bond with me. I knew I would not let the Overlord defile it. "We can't let them take this Heart," I said, my voice ringing with surprising steel. The Shard of Dawn, Heart of the Forest, and Stone of the Mountain ignited in response.

"Amareya, does the tower have any defenses left?" Kaeden asked, hope threading desperation.

"Alas, most were lost to ruin," the Priestess shook her head mournfully. "But..." Her eyes turned to the Heart of Water. "...this Heart itself is our greatest shield. If we can channel its might..."

The Nocturne fleet closed on the ruins. Warriors in obsidian armor swarmed ashore like locusts, scaling islands and rooftops. And atop the colossal flagship stood He—the Overlord himself. Flanking him like loyal hounds: Morven and Illiriy. "Looks like the Overlord brought his whole entourage this time," Kaeden observed grimly.

"We must hold them off," Amareya raised her hands, and water from the pool surged upward, weaving a dense, churning barrier around the tower. "Kaeden, Jorjen—guard the lower levels! Elara, stay with me. We'll reinforce the shield." I positioned myself beside her, channeling my Spark into the aqueous wall. It thickened, golden sparks dancing through its currents.

The assault erupted in fury. Nocturne soldiers scaled the walls with hooks of dark energy. Illiriy hurled streams of shadow magic at us. Amareya countered each onslaught, summoning colossal water lashes that swept warriors into the depths and shattered spells. I, drawing on my reserves, bolstered the shield and blasted back those who ventured too near with shafts of light.

The battle was madness. The tower trembled. Shouts, clashing steel, and the roar of magic blended into apocalyptic cacophony. "They're breaking through, child!" Amareya cried as a squad crested our platform. Without ceasing her shield-weaving, she hurled an ice lance at the nearest foe. I joined the fray, my light strikes hurling attackers into the raging abyss. But they were endless.

Suddenly, my Spark shifted—deeper, vastly more potent. I glanced at the Heart of Water. It throbbed faster, and in my mind echoed its song—not mere chimes, but words in the tongue of the First Guardians. An ancient, primal anthem of raw power. The ocean's hymn. The song of life. And I knew what to do.

"Amareya! Step back!" I shouted, otherworldly strength flooding my veins. "I'll try to unleash its true force!" The Priestess regarded me with mingled dread and hope. "Be wary, child! It could prove fatal!" I advanced to the Heart and placed both palms fearlessly on its living surface. I let its divine energy flow through me, mingling with my Spark, the power of the Stone of the Mountain, and the Heart of the Forest.

I thrust my arms skyward, and from them erupted not a mere beam, but a colossal waterspout laced with countless lightning bolts and solar flares. It crashed upon the Nocturne fleet. Screams of terror rang out. Enemy vessels spun like driftwood, splintering and dragging hundreds into the depths.

The Overlord recoiled on his flagship, rage twisting his features. He raised a hand, unleashing a bolt of inky-black lightning at my vortex. Two primordial forces—my unified light and his devouring darkness—collided in thunderous cataclysm. The tower shook. My energy waned; the Overlord remained inconceivably strong.

Then I heard him. Kaeden's voice. "Elara! Hold on! I'm with you!" He vaulted to my side in a single bound, sword defiantly aimed at the Overlord. And behind him... with joyous relief, I saw Old Finn and his crew! Somehow, they'd mended the *Sea Star* and docked at the tower to aid us!

"Didn't expect such a welcome, eh, Overlord?" Finn taunted with a mocking grin. The Overlord's face contorted in fresh fury. "Pitiful insects! You'll all perish this day!" He redoubled his assault, darkness surging toward us.

But I was no longer alone. Amareya, Kaeden, Finn, Jorjen, and his sailors formed an unbreakable phalanx. The mighty Heart of Water blazed brighter than ever. Together, as one, we met the onslaught. And this time... the all-consuming, eternal shadow faltered.

Chapter 56: Dawn over Aqualon

The Overlord's all-consuming darkness clashed against the desperate light of Aqualon's final defenders. The ancient tower's summit became an arena of apocalyptic fury.

The Overlord seethed with madness. His features twisted in bestial rage as his initial, devastating strike was boldly repelled. "Pitiful vermin!" he thundered, his voice booming over the waves. "You truly believe you can halt me?!"

He raised his arms, and from the sea's depths—summoned by his will—rose fresh, more sinister shadows: loathsome, multi-eyed abominations woven from primordial void. "Children, beware! These are servants of the Abyss itself!" Amareya cried in horror. She swept her hands, and colossal serpents of water surged from the pool, lunging at the shadowy horrors.

Kaeden, Finn, and his sailors clustered around us, fending off Nocturne warriors who had breached the platform. The air thickened with cries, the ring of steel, and the coppery tang of blood. I knew we couldn't endure much longer. The Overlord's power was inhuman. His shadow spawn tore through Amareya's watery guardians; his dark sorcery pierced our barriers.

"Elara! Focus!" Kaeden's voice cut through the tumult. He shielded me with his body from a shadow lance hurled by Illiriy from the enemy deck. "Only you can stop him!"

In desperation, I fixed my gaze on the Overlord's form. He gathered a massive orb of concentrated darkness in his palm, savoring the moment. I knew if that sphere touched the tower, nothing would remain of us. Primal fear gripped my heart. I couldn't. He was too mighty.

But then warmth bloomed from my artifacts. The Shard of Dawn, Heart of the Forest, Stone of the Mountain—they all ignited, infusing me with renewed vigor. And once more, voices whispered in my mind. The Guardians' voices. *You are not alone... We believe in you... Your light is our last hope...*

Understanding dawned. I wasn't to battle his darkness with fury of my own. I was to embody pure, all-healing radiance. Closing my eyes, I let my Spark swell, drawing in the unified essence of the three World Hearts. Within me blossomed something greater. Perfect harmony.

When I opened my eyes, I was transformed. A conduit for primordial Light. I lifted my hands, and from me poured not scorching beams, but a gentle, warm, golden glow. It enveloped the tower, the sea, the Nocturne ships.

The shadow creatures wailed in despair, unraveling not to ash, but to glistening droplets of pure water. Nocturne warriors froze, weapons clattering from numb fingers, staring in terror and awe at the impossible luminescence. Even the Overlord faltered, his arm lowering. The orb in his grasp wavered, dimming. Disbelief flickered in his starlit eyes. "What... infernal sorcery is this?!" he hissed.

"It is no sorcery, Overlord," Amareya's voice rang strong and triumphant. "It is the Light—the very Light you once betrayed."

My radiance intensified, scattering the millennia of gloom. It brushed Aqualon's ruins, and for an instant, they seemed to stir with life. It touched the wounded sailors, silencing their groans. It caressed Kaeden, easing the tension from his face, replacing it with reverent wonder.

But the Overlord refused surrender. With a savage roar, he amassed his full dark essence and hurled it at me. "Darkness always triumphs over light! That is the law of this world!"

Two primordial torrents—my light and his shadow—collided in cataclysmic thunder. It was a clash of wills, of faiths, a battle for Etheria's soul.

My strength ebbed. The Overlord remained unfathomably potent. "Elara! Hold on! Don't yield!" Kaeden's desperate cry pierced the storm.

Then the impossible unfolded. My three artifacts blazed in unison. Their primal energies fused with my Spark, forging a singular, unbreakable surge. But this was no mere light. It carried the earth's unyielding strength, the forest's ancient wisdom, the ocean's boundless might. With my last reserves, I directed it at the Overlord.

He screamed. Not just in rage, but primal terror. His darkness quivered and began to fray. His form shifted. The sinister robes dissolved, revealing... something long forgotten. Achingly familiar. I glimpsed his true face. Incredibly young. Beautiful. Etched with inexpressible torment. The face from my visions—the man he had been before his fall.

"No... this cannot be..." he mouthed silently, staring in horror at hands regaining human flesh. My light fully enshrouded his trembling figure. For a heartbeat, the eternal shadow in his eyes receded, yielding to... belated remorse. Then he simply vanished. Dissolved into that all-forgiving glow.

Deprived of their leader, the Nocturne ships faltered in disarray. Slowly, warily, they retreated northward. I sank to my knees, heavy with exhaustion. The light around me began to fade. The harrowing battle was over.

Chapter 57: Dawn of New Hope

The all-encompassing light from the united World Hearts slowly ebbed, yielding to a resonant silence and the crisp scent of sea breeze. I sank heavily onto the damp stones, gripped by utter exhaustion yet suffused with otherworldly serenity.

The Overlord had vanished. Utterly. Dissolved into that all-forgiving radiance. Was it annihilation? Or an inconceivable redemption? I could not say. Bereft of their master, the Nocturne ships fled in panic, their sable sails fading beyond the horizon. The battle for Aqualon was over. We had triumphed.

Kaeden, bloodied but unbreakable, rushed to my side. "Elara... you... you did it," he whispered, his voice quivering. Amareya, the last Priestess, approached next, luminous tears in her eyes. "The Almighty Light has prevailed over Shadow, my valiant child. You have fulfilled the most arduous verse of the ancient prophecy."

Old Finn and his surviving sailors—including the wounded but unbowed Jorjen—watched in reverent hush. "What became of him?" I managed, my words scraping from a parched throat.

"I do not know, dear Elara," Amareya replied, shaking her head. "Perhaps your light cleansed his tormented soul. Or he returned to the void from which he once emerged."

We lingered in silence, gazing at the calming sea. Dawn broke, painting Aqualon's ruins in tender rose hues. For the first time in centuries, the ancient city seemed to exhale in relief. The canal waters cleared, and fragile green shoots pierced the stones. The Heart of Water on its pedestal glowed with steady, soothing light, its crystalline song now fluid and lullaby-soft.

But victory came at steep cost. Two sailors lay lost. Captain Finn bore a gash in his shoulder; Kaeden's old wound had reopened. Yet we endured.

In the days that followed, we turned to renewal. Amareya, drawing on the Heart of Water's power, began mending Aqualon. I aided as best I could, learning from the wise Priestess long-forgotten arts of water magic. Kaeden and the sailors repaired our battered *Sea Star*. We spoke at length—of the Overlord, our path ahead, Etheria's fate.

"Even if he's gone," Kaeden said one evening as we sat by the shore, "his dark legacy lingers—Nocturne, his minions, the Gloom Blight. Our fight is just beginning."

"I know," I replied softly. "The ancient voice said I must not only awaken the World Hearts but unite them. We've roused three. But one remains... the last... the Heart of the Heavens."

"The legendary Heart of the Heavens," Amareya murmured, approaching unheard, her gaze lifting to the sky. "Legends whisper it lies hidden atop the Dragon's Teeth, in a lost monastery of air mages. But none know if it truly endures."

"We must try," I said, resolve hardening like forged steel. "It's our only hope." Kaeden met my eyes, faith unwavering in his. "I'll stand with you always, Elara. Wherever you lead."

"Well, children," Old Finn grunted, joining us with a wry grin, "if our Child of the Spark sets forth again, the *Sea Star* is hers to command. Can't miss all the excitement!" He winked at Jorjen with infectious mirth.

Thus, on the shores of reborn Aqualon, our new vow was sealed. Our quest: the legendary Heart of the Heavens.

Weeks later, with the *Sea Star* seaworthy and our wounds knit, we bade Amareya a heartfelt farewell. "May the eternal Light of the Guardians guide your way," she said, embracing me like a mother. "Remember, Elara, true power lies not in destruction, but creation. In harmony with all that is." She pressed a pouch of fragrant herbs into my hand. "These will serve you in the mountains. They'll ward off the wind's icy grasp."

We boarded the deck of our faithful *Sea Star*. She turned northward, toward the snow-capped Dragon's Teeth. I stood at the prow beside Kaeden, the vast sea stretching before us. The journey would be long and perilous. But I was no longer alone. I had steadfast companions. A noble, sacred purpose. And an extraordinary strength—the power of Light, of Love, of Hope.

I knew, deep in my heart, I believed with every fiber: this time, we would prevail. Together. The milky-white Shard of Dawn at my throat, as if affirming my resolve, pulsed faintly but surely, its invisible beam charting our course—to fresh adventures, new trials, the bright future we would wrest from eternal darkness. Our scarred Etheria awaited healing. And we, her last children, were already on our way.

End of Book One